DEVOURER OF SOULS

SOPHAN
&
THE MAN IN YELLOW

KEVIN LUCIA

D1264565

Crystal Lake Publishing
www.CrystalLakePub.com

OTHER TITLES BY KEVIN LUCIA
THROUGH
CRYSTAL LAKE PUBLISHING

Through a Mirror, Darkly

Things Slip Through

OTHER TITLES BY CRYSTAL LAKE PUBLISHING

Tales from The Lake Vol.1

Tales from The Lake Vol.2

Pretty Little Dead Girls: A Novel of Murder and Whimsy by Mercedes M. Yardley

Apocalyptic Montessa and Nuclear Lulu: A Tale of Atomic Love by Mercedes M. Yardley

Wind Chill by Patrick Rutigliano

Eidolon Avenue: The First Feast by Jonathan Winn

Flowers in a Dumpster by Mark Allan Gunnells

Nameless: The Darkness Comes by Mercedes M. Yardley

The Dark at the End of the Tunnel by Taylor Grant

Writers On Writing: An Author's Guide

Or check out other Crystal Lake Publishing books for your Dark Fiction, Horror, Suspense, and Thriller needs, and join our newsletter while you're there.

DEVOURER OF SOULS

THE SKYLARK DINER

WHEN FATHER WARD enters I can tell by his expression that something heavy is weighing on his mind. In and of itself that isn't unusual. As priest at All Saints Church and Headmaster of All Saints Academy he's got a pretty full plate. Preoccupied seems his constant mental state these days. If he didn't love his work so much I'd worry about it a little, honestly.

Truthfully, in spite of how much he enjoys both his vocations, I *do* worry, but not about him burning out. Father Ward's got a good head on his shoulders and a healthy dose of common sense. He knows when and how far to push himself, and when to relax. Plus, he served time in Afghanistan as an Army Chaplain. He saw some pretty rough action (though he's never shared the exact details) and he survived just fine. You don't manage that without some serious steel in your spine.

No, it's not Father Ward's busy work schedule that concerns me.

It's this town, and the strange things that hide here.

See, for whatever reason—Fate, Destiny, Providence, Blind Dumb Luck, Losing the Cosmic Sweepstakes—my friends and I have been chosen as the ones who get to know all the dark little secrets of this town. We don't look for them or seek them out. They come to us. Like iron filings to magnets, these secrets and stories and half-truths come to us in many different ways. In fact, one of them is sitting before me on my booth's table, now.

And this one seems meant especially for Bill Ward, priest of All Saints Church and Headmaster at All Saints Academy.

∽∞∾

Soon as Father Ward nears my booth that preoccupied look vanishes, replaced by his customary, easy-going smile. "Morning, Chris. *Sheriff.* You order yet?"

I shake my head, smiling in return, which is almost impossible *not* to do, despite the occasion bringing us to The Skylark this morning. "Was waiting for you. Figured we could eat *after.*"

I nod at the plain, black-cloth journal (the kind found in almost any bookstore) sitting on the table. Father Ward's smile fades slightly as he slides into the booth across from me. "Ah. I see. So this is one of *those* breakfasts."

"Afraid so. But it's been pretty quiet around here lately, so . . . guess we had to expect it sooner or later."

"True enough. Gavin and Fitzy coming?"

Fitzy-Mike Fitzgerald—is an MD at Utica General Hospital and Gavin Patchett is a mid-list genre novelist turned high school English teacher who only recently started writing again, releasing a collection of

4

short stories through a small publisher titled *Things Slip Through*. We all met through Gavin. Several years ago one of his students was involved in a shooting. I was the first officer on the scene. Fitzy treated the shooter at the hospital. Father Ward counseled her before she went to The Riverdale Center downstate for treatment. Through that tragedy bonds of tentative friendship formed. We began meeting regularly and soon Poker Tuesdays became a mainstay, as has breakfast or lunch or dinner at The Skylark, schedules permitting.

Unfortunately, not all our gatherings are for pleasure. But such is the way of things, and we've come to accept that.

"No. Fitzy just finished pulling a double shift at the hospital, so he's sleeping. Gavin's out of town, at a writing convention down Binghamton way."

Father Ward's smile widens at this. "Ah, yes. How's the collection faring?"

"According to Gavin, getting good reviews and selling well. He's happy. Seems more at peace these days. I think that's all he cares about, really."

And that's the truest thing you can say. Gavin's full-time writing career ended badly. Too much drinking, too much hype, a near-fatal car accident, and he called it quits seven years ago. He returned to Clifton Heights and for the next five years drifted through a teaching career at the public school, barely getting by and still drinking too much. Two years ago his student was involved in that shooting. Afterward he quit drinking and began writing again . . .

Though not necessarily because he wanted to. Not at *first*, anyway. Like those iron filings we all seem to attract, he started writing stories about the things that happen in this town when no one's looking; the things that lurk in the dark corners everyone else would rather ignore.

Do these stories really happen?

There's no way of knowing. Initially this uncertainty tormented him. He didn't sleep well for a long while. However, publishing some of them in *Things Slip Through* has given him a measure of peace. Helped him embrace his . . . calling, if you will, just like we have.

I grapple with cases that can't be solved. Father Ward hears the strangest confessions, though he can't share the specifics about most of them. Fitzy—even though he works in Utica—treats John and Jane Doe patients who often disappear afterward.

Gavin? He writes unexplainable stories that may or may not be true. Like I said: iron filings to our magnets.

And unfortunately, it's time to quit stalling and deal with the latest iron filing attracted our way. I place a hand on the journal and look at Father Ward, trying to keep my expression neutral. "Couple days ago folks living on Upper Bassler Road called in reports of strange lights at night."

Father Ward's eyebrows lift slightly. "Bassler House?"

Bassler House is an old abandoned Victorian farmhouse sitting in the middle of a fallow cornfield off Bassler Road, on the edge of town. We've heard our fair share of stories about that place. Everyone has. Every small town needs its own spook house, right?

"No. Further up the road, closer to the Commons

Trailer Park. Sent one of my deputies—Freddy Potter— to investigate. Turned out to be a high-powered flashlight someone left on, under that old Oriental gazebo out there. The one in that overgrown flower garden near those rows of blueberry bushes. You know where I'm talking about?"

Surprised recognition dawns in Father Ward's eyes. "Yeah. Mr. Trung's old place. Nice Vietnamese guy from when I was a kid. Retired. Raised blueberry and raspberry bushes. Everybody picked berries there. His flower garden was something else, too. Sad the way he died, all alone like that."

He frowns. Glances down at the journal, then back up at me. "Did you find this . . . ?"

I nod, tapping the journal. "I took it home, read it." I look at Father Ward closely. "You remember a Nate Slocum?"

Father Ward sits back against the booth's cushions, looking thoughtful. "Sure. Good guy. We weren't super friends, but we shared the same taste in movies. Always used to watch those old 'Creature Features' that played at Raedeker Park back in the day. After college, I guess he came home to live with his dad, right? Been working at the lumber mill since?"

I sigh and push the journal toward Father Ward. "Not anymore."

SOPHAN

ONE

MY CHILDHOOD FRIEND Jake Burns is getting pretty upset, stomping and waving next to what's left of Mr. Trung's koi pond. I'm sitting nearby, writing this beneath an old Oriental-style gazebo, which looks just like I remember as a kid, except its white paint has faded with time. Honestly, I can't believe it's still standing after all these years.

The koi pond hasn't fared nearly as well. Its concrete border is cracked and crumbling. Water lilies clog its scummy surface. And I have to wonder. Have the koi somehow survived the years? Do they still live and breed in the pond's depths? Are they still waiting, after all this time, for Mr. Trung to wade into the water, hands upraised, chanting . . . ?

No.

I don't want to think about that. I don't want to be here, either.

Neither does Jake. He'd beaten me here, was standing over the spot where he once destroyed an old stone chest with a hand-sledge. As I'd thrashed my way through overgrown weeds he'd waved me off, clear from his agonized expression that he desperately wanted me to run away.

But it's too late for that, now.

This was set into motion long ago, dictated by forces much larger than me. I've anticipated tonight for the last twenty years. My expectations came true yesterday when I received my package in the mail. Soon as I opened it, I knew the time had come to finally face my fate.

So I ignored Jake (which is easy if I don't look at him, because he can't speak), cleared a spot on the gazebo's third step, sat, opened the cardboard box and pulled out its contents: an antique-looking wooden chest painted a deep black. On the lid, etched and inlaid with silver is an exotic, oriental character I've come to know far too well.

But I can't open it just yet. Someone needs to know what really happened to Jake Burns.

And I *need* to tell it . . .

TWO

J AKE BURNS NEVER really fit in, no matter how hard he tried. He made crude jokes no one laughed at and possessed few manners. His temper flared at a moment's notice, bringing a dangerous glint to his eyes. Quite frankly, he was also disgusting, even for an adolescent boy. He burped and farted and picked his nose with reckless abandon, regardless of the company he was in.

He wasn't all bad, though. He could knock a mean line drive down center field (which made him useful during Little League season) and he always found the best fishing holes. But I think we all knew in our hearts Jake was headed for a bad end. We figured he'd do time in the county jail someday for something stupid or that his hair-trigger temper would get him knifed in a bar somewhere.

Why did we tolerate him always tagging along?

Probably because we felt sorry for him. Jake's dad beat him relentlessly. Beat him when drunk, when sober, or just on principal when he suspected Jake was "sassing" him.

We never talked about it. He never said a word, and we never asked. That's just how things were, especially in a small town where everyone knew everything about each other but liked to pretend they didn't. It was the late eighties, and small towns were small towns. Some things weren't talked about and, being kids, there wasn't much we could do about it. Besides, Jake wasn't technically a "friend." He was just always . . . *there*.

But we knew what was going on.

When Jake showed up to Little League practice with his cap pulled down to hide his shiner. When we noticed the small burns on his knuckles while out fishing. When he lagged behind us on his bike one day because he'd "hurt his back" chopping wood.

We knew.

And because of this I don't think my friends were really surprised when he disappeared. They took it in stride, guessing he'd finally had it with his old man and split.

Only I knew differently, but I never said so. I kept my mouth shut and played it straight, agreeing with them.

But something *else* had happened.

Jake hadn't run away. Something had taken him and only I knew who was responsible. Mr. Trung, the kindly old Oriental man who lived on Bassler Road in a modest double-wide trailer with his manicured lawn, thick blueberry bushes, lush flower garden, and koi pond.

It was at Mr. Trung's where I last saw Jake Burns.

It was there I heard him scream.

THREE

"HERE HE COMES," Kevin Ellison muttered as we browsed over a table filled with used comic books at the Commons Trailer Park Yard Sale. I glanced up and, sure enough, there was Jake Burns peddling his clunky old bike down the fairway toward us.

I snorted and returned my attention to an issue of *Rom: Space Knight.* "Peachy."

"Y'know, he *really* seems to dig you," whispered Gary McNamara from the other side of the table, where he was perusing an issue of *Thor.* "I mean *really*. Like you're best buds or something."

I shook my head and sighed, trying to lose myself in Rom battling these blobby aliens whose tongues turned into drills that bored into a person's skull and ate their brains so the aliens could *become* them. It was a little cruel but as Jake clattered to a stop I wondered if that's why he didn't fit in. Maybe he was like one of these aliens. After eating the brains of the "real" Jake Burns a few years ago, he'd never learned how to act like the rest of us.

His sneering grin exposed slightly yellow teeth. "How's it hanging, *bitches*?"

15

Kevin, standing next to me and rummaging through some old issues of *The Hulk*, murmured, "If we're bitches, then *nothing* is hanging, Jake."

I snorted and glanced at Jake. As usual, when one of his one-liners fell flat he just looked confused. "Screw off, Ellison. Why dontcha go dribble your balls somewhere?"

Kevin's laugh was quiet but somehow gentle. He was easily the kindest of us, definitely kinder than me. Why couldn't have Jake latched onto *him* instead?

Of course, Kevin was too different. He got good grades; read a lot, played basketball, had both parents and an older sister who excelled at track and cross country. Plus, his dad taught English at All Saints, the Catholic School across town.

My dad and Jake's were more alike, however. They'd grown up together out in the hills, fought in Vietnam together and had worked together at the lumber mill until Jake's dad got fired last month for showing up drunk once too often. They both enjoyed the stock car races at Five Mile Speedway, occasionally hunted together and had both lost their wives.

So I suppose Jake felt closer to me than anyone else, maybe even thought we were connected somehow. I did my best to humor him but it was hard because I couldn't shake him. He was *always* there. For whatever reason, Jake had clearly picked me as his favorite, and that wasn't changing anytime soon.

"So whatcha all lookin at?" He leered over the table hopefully. I swear he licked his lips. "Titty mags?"

"Nope," said Gary, "but I think I saw some Playgirls somewhere. Ain't that your thing?"

Jake scowled. Real anger flashed in his eyes. He

clashed with Gary a lot. Gary's dad was a lawyer, school board member and a deacon at the Baptist church. Mr. McNamara had butted heads with Jake's dad over many things. It was rumored that Mr. McNamara was the only person brave (or stupid) enough to report Jake's dad to Webb County Protective Services. Jake and Gary picked up the vibes between their fathers and bad blood had always simmered there.

"Suck it, Macky. Don't need no Playgirls cause I got naked pictures of your *momma*."

Gary made a noise in the back of his throat, dropped *Thor* and muttered, "Whatever. You guys deal with him. I'm not in the mood today."

Jake frowned as Gary moved away. "Oh, c'mon Macky. I was only kiddin'! Don't be such a fuckin' baby!"

And that was Jake right down to the ground. He'd say something crude or offensive, then wouldn't understand when someone got pissed. Again, like an alien who'd never quite learned how to act human.

Gary's only response was to flip Jake the bird over his shoulder as he left. Jake snorted and waved. "Whatever. Baby. Like anyone'd wanna see his mom naked anyway."

Jake turned and offered us his crooked grin again, a little more carefree and a little less malicious, which of course meant one thing. "So, we goin' fishin' today or what?"

"I dunno," Kevin said. "Maybe."

I shrugged, but we were merely delaying the inevitable. The only way to get rid of Jake Burns was to hang out with him for as long as we could stand, then claim pressing engagements elsewhere. That was the way of things. Sadly, he lapped it up like a dog dying of thirst.

"Bullshit. Ain't that your fishin' gear sittin' out front next to your bikes?"

Luckily, I at least had an excuse for leaving early. "Yeah, but I gotta ditch before noon. Amy nagged me into stopping at Mr. Trung's for some blueberries on the way home."

"I've got basketball over at the Utica Y tonight, so I have to leave early, too," Kevin added smoothly. As usual, his excuses slipped gently into the conversation.

But Jake ignored Kevin's excuse and spat on the ground. "Mr. *Trung*. Fuckin' gook bastard. Get blueberries somewhere else, why dontcha? Wouldn't trust that gook sumbitch with my fuckin' *shit*."

I glanced up from *Rom* and, as always, shivered a little at Jake's reaction to Mr. Trung. He'd *always* hated the old guy. It was weird because Jake had never seemed racist or anything. Clifton Heights was (and still is) a small Adirondack country town, mostly white. However, a few black folks and Indians lived in and around town and Jake didn't seem to mind them at all. The year before, he'd taken no notice of our Chinese exchange student.

Why he hated Mr. Trung none of us knew. A while ago, Kevin had made the connection between Mr. Trung's nationality (Vietnamese) and Jake's dad fighting in Vietnam. But my dad fought in Vietnam, too. He liked Mr. Trung just fine, said his blueberries were the best.

So like everyone else, I felt no sympathy for Jake's unexplained wrath. "C'mon, Jake. Nothing's wrong with Mr. Trung. He's a nice old guy who's got the best blueberries around. Plus, if we're hitting Black Creek Mr. Trung's place is on the way home."

"Well fine," he mumbled. "Y'all can quit early. I'll just stay'n keep fishin.'"

Of course, he wouldn't do that. If we left early he'd tag along, even if we stopped at the hated Mr. Trung's, because he clung to us like crazy glue. Again, it was only years later that I fully understood: as rough, crude and unpleasant as Jake was, he couldn't stand being alone.

A few minutes of silence passed. Kevin and I read comics while Jake straddled his bike, industriously picking his nose. Then we heard:

"Hey, girls. What's shaking?"

We turned to see three guys our age approaching. The one who spoke was a redhead named Mike Fitzgerald. Everyone knew him as Fitzy. He played basketball with Kevin. Second was Fitzy's best friend since Kindergarten, Bill Ward, and the third was Gavin Patchett, whom I didn't know very well. He was new. Moved here two years ago.

Fitzy slapped Kevin's shoulder and nodded at me, smart enough (like most everyone else) to ignore Jake. "So what's up? Perusing the fine assortment of treasures here at the Commons Yard Sale?"

Kevin shrugged. "Yeah, for a bit. Gonna fish a little after."

Fitzy clapped Kevin on the shoulder and said with a brilliant grin, "Ditch the fish and come with. We're initiating old Gavin here. Finally making him an *official* townie."

Kevin and I groaned. Fitzy meant they were off to

explore old Bassler House, a rundown Victorian farmhouse out in the middle of an old cornfield just down the road. Every small town has a 'haunted house' and I suppose Bassler House was ours. Every boy (and a few intrepid girls) in town had braved Bassler House once or twice. In the end, even though it had a spooky vibe, it was just an old abandoned house and nothing else.

Fitzy mock-scowled. "Oh, c'mon. Set a good example for Gavin, why dontcha?"

Kevin shook his head and grinned. "Nope. Been there and done that, Fitzy. We're good."

Bill, who'd been quiet up until then, smiled at me and said, "Creature from the Black Lagoon is showing Wednesday night at the park, Nate. You down?"

I grinned. "Yeah, definitely."

"Cool. If you get there first, save me a spot."

Fitzy snorted, rolling his eyes. "But don't you Holy Rollin' Baptists got church Wednesdays?"

Bill shook his head, wearing a long-suffering look of patience. "Youth group is out for the summer."

"Oh, well. Thank goodness for that. How could you stand to miss all that praying and singing and *hallelulah!* Praise the Lord! *Anyway*," he flipped us a jaunty two-fingered salute, "we're off to brave the dread mysteries of Bassler House. If we don't come back, remember us, okay?"

I grinned. "Sure. I'll even inscribe your tombstone. It'll say: 'Here Lies Fitzy, Who Died of Embarrassment over Pissing Himself When He Jumped at a Shadow.'"

"Nice. Very touching, numb-nuts." He spun away, grinning ear to ear. "All right. Enjoy the yard sale. Treat yourselves to something nice, ladies. I think there's some cute little girl skirts in aisle five."

SOPHAN

They waved and left to the sound of our catcalls and booing. I tossed my issue of *Rom* back onto the table. "All right. Where's Gary? We wanna get any fishing done before I hit Mr. Trung's, we gotta get going."

"Still don't know why you wanna stop at that stupid gook's place. He probably poisons them berries of his."

Jake's snarl startled me. I'd completely forgotten he was there. That happened a lot, partly because he clammed up when others came around, but also because we usually did our best to ignore him.

Kevin sighed patiently, offering Jake a very parental look of quiet exasperation. "Obviously not or else the whole town would be dead by now, seeing as how pretty much *everyone* picks their blueberries there, Jake."

Jake's scowl twisted his face into an ugly expression that chilled me, despite the summer heat. "Not me, no sir. Me an' my Pa ain't buyin' nothin' from that gook sumbitch. No way, not a chance in hell."

I shook my head, trying to ignore how uneasy his gleaming eyes made me. "Stow it, Jake."

Jake's eyes flashed. His lip curled. "Why? He's a stinkin' gook bastard who—"

"All right. *Enough.*"

Jake blinked at Kevin's flat command. Even I glanced at him, a little surprised at his tone, though I suppose I shouldn't have been. Kevin didn't often get mad but like everyone else he had a line. Usually anything like racism or prejudice pushed him over it.

"We get it, Jake. You don't like Mr. Trung. Let's *stop* now, okay? Or we can go fishing without you from now on."

Silence.

Jake looked shocked and maybe a little awed. All the nastiness fled his face, red freckles burning against his suddenly pale skin as he stammered, "Geez, Kev . . . I'm sorry, I didn't mean . . . honest . . . "

Kevin shook his head. "We're done, okay? No more about Mr. Trung."

"Okay. Shit, yeah. I was just . . . I mean, I was just . . . okay, yeah, shit yeah, no more."

Kevin nodded. I spoke quickly, trying to defuse the tension that had built so suddenly between us. "Where's Gary? Never gonna get any fishing done at this rate."

Kevin turned and peered down the fairway deeper into the Commons. "Dunno. Probably should track him down, though." He tossed down his issue of *The Hulk* and moved away, deeper into the yard sale. We followed him.

The Commons Yard Sale boasted a pretty impressive spread of assorted novelties and knickknacks. About twenty years ago the Commons served as home for white trash, squatters, hippies and more than a few druggies. But according to my dad it came under new ownership in the seventies and got mostly cleaned up.

The yard sale started about five or six years ago. A few folks living in the Commons decided to hold yard sales at the same time, putting signs out on Bassler Road. They did that for a few years and lots of people came. Pretty soon almost every trailer put a table up, selling all sorts of things. Kids living in the Commons took advantage of the crowds and sold lemonade and homemade cookies. Then one year the trailer park owner Phil Seward broke out his grill and hotdogs and Shasta and Penguin Soda. A year later he got the bright idea of letting townies set up tables along the fairway for a small fee, and the Commons Yard Sale was born.

We always found the neatest things there. If you've been to many yard sales you know what I'm talking about. Some tables offered nothing but boring grown-up junk, like tools or plates or old drinking glasses. Other tables, though, boasted stacks of board games and children's books, boxes of action figures, Legos, Lincoln Logs, and all the useless things kids *loved*.

Like tins filled with assorted colored beads, marbles and rubber bands. Vintage soda bottles, like the kinds Kevin collected. Bottle caps and plastic buildings for model train sets. We wasted most of our meager allowances there and never once regretted it because the Commons Yard Sale offered everything imaginable.

In fact, we might've spent the whole day there and never gone fishing at all (despite Jake's urging) if we hadn't come across Mr. Trung. We'd worked our way to a table with a bunch of hand-held electronic games. You remember—the ones with green LED lights that *blipped* over black screens and were nearly impossible to play? I was trying to figure out how to pass on a football game while Kevin was tinkering with a hand-held basketball game. Jake had been playing some sort of baseball game but it wasn't long before he lost patience, rudely dropped it onto the table and moved on.

That's when I heard it.

A soft, cultured and intelligent voice with just the slightest accent.

A voice I'll never forget as long as I live.

"Hello, Master Jake. Good to see you again. How are you this fine day?"

Mr. Trung.

I looked up from the football game to see Jake standing motionless before Mr. Trung's table, feet rooted to the ground . . . looking afraid, of all things. While Kevin rummaged in his pocket for a few bucks to buy the basketball game, I tossed the football game onto the table and joined Jake, a little surprised by a vague concern . . .

No.

That wasn't it, exactly.

It was *fear*. I was *afraid* for Jake, though I had no idea why. Such an unexpectedly empathetic notion felt strange, indeed.

Mr. Trung saw me and smiled kindly. "Ah, Master Nate. So good to see you." He nodded at Kevin, who had joined us. "And you also, Master Kevin. How is your father doing? Well, I hope?"

About ten years ago Kevin's dad helped Mr. Trung with his English so he could pass his citizenry test. Because of that, Mr. Trung always let Kevin's family pick from his blueberry patch for free. He and Mr. Ellison had remained good friends. They and my dad occasionally went fishing together.

But never with Jake's dad.

I wondered if that had anything to do with Jake's hatred of Mr. Trung, though he didn't appear so hateful, now. More like scared witless.

Either not noticing Jake or playing it straight, Kevin said, "Yeah, Dad's good. Happy it's summer, though. Had some rough classes this year, I guess."

SOPHAN

Mr. Trung's small eyes twinkled in amusement. He waved dismissively. "Bah. I'm sure he had them—how do you say?—eating from his hand by the end of the year."

Kevin laughed. "Yeah, I guess. Kids always seem to like his classes. But he's just Dad to me, so . . . "

"Of course. One often forgets that their parents have other faces besides the one they show us every day . . . "

He turned and looked at Jake, his expression suddenly blank, unreadable. "Isn't that right, Master Burns?"

Jake shivered and blinked rapidly, as if waking from a bad dream. "Huh? Uh . . . yeah. Whatever. Guess so." He turned toward me but kept his eyes on Mr. Trung, as if afraid to look away. "Let's get outta here, man. Fish're waitin.'"

"Yes, the fish," Mr. Trung continued, voice emotionless, face still weirdly blank. "Master Burns has quite the skill, doesn't he? Has a knack for knowing where things hide. Much like his *father*."

A chill crept down my neck. Mr. Trung had always acted polite and kind to us. This bland look and odd manner seemed so . . . alien.

And it hit me.

Taunting.

He was taunting Jake. Needling and prodding him about something.

But what?

Something's wrong, whispered a little voice inside my head. *Why is Mr. Trung acting so weird? Why is Jake* afraid *of him?*

I had no answers but now felt as uneasy as Jake

looked. I glanced at Kevin again and tried to sound relaxed. "Y'know, Jake's right. We should get going."

Kevin opened his mouth to reply but before he could say anything Mr. Trung said, "Please, before you go, boys. I have some very special things for sale this morning. If something catches your eye . . . "

For some odd reason I didn't want to look at his table. But it was Mr. Trung, after all. Kind, gentle, amiable Mr. Trung, who always offered a warm smile to everyone. There couldn't possibly be anything harmful there. Whatever Jake feared, it had to be in his imagination.

When I looked down, I immediately felt stupid. There wasn't anything to be afraid of. Just the usual types of yard sale items, though with a decidedly Oriental bent. Jade figurines of tigers and dragons, paper fans with Chinese calligraphy on them, small little statues, and polished jade spheres.

"See anything that strikes your . . . what do you call it . . . ? fancy, boys?"

When I raised my head to say, "No," my mouth dropped open a little. His *eyes*. Mr. Trung's eyes looked like little pools of glimmering black oil. It looked like he was *hungry,* and he wasn't looking at me or Kevin at all . . .

He was staring at Jake like Kevin and I didn't exist. "Anything, boys?"

I looked back down and frowned, seeing something I hadn't before. A small, rectangular black box made of smooth wood with intricate, silver-embossed designs engraved into the top. It looked old and worth a lot of money, not something you'd find at a yard sale.

I pointed. "What's that?"

SOPHAN

Though I could've sworn my ears were playing tricks on me, I thought I heard Jake rasp, "No. *Please.*"

Something passed over Mr. Trung's face when I spoke. A slight frown, as if he were unhappy *I* had asked about the box instead of Jake.

But, prodded by curiosity, I coughed and spoke a little louder. "What is it, Mr. Trung?"

Mr. Trung shook his head slightly as he faced me, as if disappointed in something. When he smiled, however, some of his strange spookiness seeped away; leaving the nice old man I'd known my whole life.

"A game, Master Nate," he said, delicate-looking fingers gently lifting the lid. "A game and, according to legend, much more."

He opened the box, revealing neat stacks of shining white, polished ivory squares inscribed with exotic designs that looked like the calligraphy. Except these looked different, somehow. I certainly couldn't read them but they didn't look right, though I couldn't say how.

Kevin whistled. "Neat. What's it called?"

Mr. Trung glanced sideways at Jake, almost as if he expected *him* to answer, but maybe for the first time ever since I'd known him Jake Burns had nothing to say.

Mr. Trung spoke while still gazing at Jake, his face unreadable. "It's a game reaching back generations to the Ancients of my people. Its purest name is 'Sốphận.' It means *fate.*"

Ever the sportsman, Kevin asked what he obviously thought was the most pertinent question. "How do you play? Like . . . how do you *win*?"

Mr. Trung folded his hands before him and looked

27

at me, then returned his gaze to Jake, narrowing his eyes a little, as if measuring him. "Really, 'game' isn't quite right. There are winners and losers but it's also a test that reveals character, uncovers secrets hid beneath the surface, revealing destinies that are to be."

"You mean like the Magic Eight Ball?" Kevin deadpanned, smiling slightly.

Amazingly all the eeriness seeped out of Mr. Trung. He offered a kind smile and replied in a much lighter tone, "In a way, though it is much more accurate. There are no tiles for 'Ask Again Later' or 'Future is Hazy,' you see."

Both Kevin and I chuckled at this. I felt some of my unease fading, though I still sensed Jake's fear.

"All of this, of course, is a legend handed down for generations." He gestured casually at the opened box and those gleaming white tiles inscribed with those exotic designs. "Really, it is now nothing more than a curious pastime, a clever . . . how does one say . . . parlor goof?"

"Parlor trick," Kevin offered.

Mr. Trung laughed. It was the same laugh I'd known my whole life: relaxed, unrestrained, slightly cackling and somehow musical at once. He clapped his hands and nodded. "Yes, yes, that is it. An intriguing parlor trick, nothing more."

Next to me, this time I *knew* Jake whispered, "That's not *true*."

I glanced at him but had to force my gaze back to Mr. Trung because I'd never seen Jake like that: completely intimidated. As I looked at Mr. Trung and met his gaze, I saw something flash there . . .

And somehow I *knew*. I didn't understand *how* I knew, but I did.

Mr. Trung was *lying*.

The game was a lot more than a 'parlor goof' and not only was he hiding that from us, but also . . . Jake somehow knew the game was more, too.

I piped up. "How'dya play? Can you show us?"

Again, an innocent smile from Mr. Trung. "You don't play this for sport or money, like Mahjong. According to the Ancients, you don't play against an earthly opponent at all . . . you play against Sõphận, or Fate, itself."

Kevin nodded slowly, looking thoughtful. "Okay," he said. "What's the *object* of the game?"

Mr. Trung's smile widened. He looked very pleased as he raised a finger. "Ah. Now *that* is the correct question."

Mr. Trung proceeded to gently remove several tiles from the box. They *clinked* together lightly as he spoke. "The legends of my people say that these tiles were made from the bones of high priests who served Khong-Lo, the god whom—according to our Legends— separated the sky and the earth. He then erected four columns to support the sky. To guard those columns, Khong-Lo created four sacred beasts."

Without looking at either of us, Mr. Trung laid down one tile, which sported a finely inscribed image of a dragon. "Long, the Sacred Dragon, guards the Eastern Column."

The next tile's engraving depicted something that looked like a tiger crossed with a lizard. "Lan, the Haunter of the Wastes, guards the Western Column."

The next was a turtle of some kind. "Quy," Mr. Trung whispered, "who guards the Northern Column."

The last looked like an eagle or vulture. "And

Phung, the Sky Hunter, guards the Southern Column."

Mr. Trung looked up at us, face too somber for a summer morning at a community yard sale. "The *object* of the game, Master Kevin, is to reach enlightenment, the Gateway to Understanding. That is what a player hopes to *win*."

Without taking his eyes off us, he laid down another tile offering two plain, etched-in-black characters . . .

"This means 'gateway.' It is what Sốphận players seek, the Gateway to Understanding."

Kevin folded his arms, looking interested. "Understanding? Of what?"

Mr. Trung smiled but it wasn't his same, kindly-old man expression. This smile seemed enigmatic . . . maybe even a little threatening. "Of everything, Master Kevin. Understanding of the self, of the surrounding world. Of the Ancients, even the universe. But the Gateway is guarded by the Four Sacred Beasts and one . . . other. Encountering any of these in the course of the game carries great consequences. According to myth, of course."

Jake said nothing but shifted uneasily next to me. Again, it struck me as an oddly amazing thing that he'd remained quiet for so long.

I looked at Mr. Trung. "Consequences?"

Mr. Trung looked at me. Again his eyes glimmered like bottomless black pools. He gently touched Long, the dragon, with his fingertip. "If you encounter Long, he shall consume you with fire." Next, he touched the iguana-tiger thing. "Lan will rend your body limb from limb. Quy will drag you to a watery grave. Phung will steal your spirit to the heavens, leaving an empty husk here to wander the Earth."

For an eerie moment, the yard sale disappeared. I didn't hear kids running around and screaming at the top of their lungs, didn't hear the murmuring chatter of the milling crowds, didn't hear dogs or birds or even cars driving on Bassler Road. For a moment there was nothing but Mr. Trung and his strange, resonant voice. The unease I'd felt only moments before returned.

Kevin grunted. "You said something about an 'Other.'"

Oddly enough, Mr. Trung looked regretful at that, as if he didn't want to show us the other tile he held. "Yes." He nodded slowly, then laid the tile down next to the others.

I looked at it. My unease grew, because it looked like a bullfrog crossed with a man. Oddly enough, it looked like . . . The creature from the Black Lagoon.

"The 'Other' is Chiao, the Water Demon. According to legend he capsized boats, devoured men, and ravished women. He was . . . different from the Sacred Four."

I cleared my suddenly dry and tight throat. "How?"

Mr. Trung tipped his head. "The Four exact a price for attempting to reach the Gateway, but they are sacred, honorable, bearing your essence away to be judged accordingly. Chiao is an Abomination. It *consumes* your very essence, making you part of it for all eternity."

31

A whisper, from Kevin. "How do you play?"

Without ceremony, Mr. Trung tipped the box and dumped the rest of the tiles onto the table. He began stacking them with deft movements. "Legend has it that once the tiles are put into play they become imbued with Khong-Lo's essence, pitting the player against him . . . against Fate."

As he talked, Mr. Trung's pile grew into a strangely angled yet oddly-symmetrical pyramid. "To enter through the Gateway of Understanding you must collect eleven matching pairs of tiles, twenty-two tiles in all. You must match four Wind tiles—from the north, south, east and west—four Season tiles in spring, summer, fall, and winter, and three Dragon tiles; red, green and white. Red stands for courage, green stands for prosperity, and white stands for purity."

Kevin nodded, eying Mr. Trung's movements intently, fully in the grip of his love for competition, especially against something as ephemeral as *fate*. "So it's a matching game, then."

"Yes, but you can lose your matches along the way. That's part of the game's mystical legend: that the tiles shift and change because they *read* you. As you play, they come to know your fears and dreams and strengths and weaknesses."

He paused and held up a blank tile. "Legend says that these blank tiles—called Nha tiên tri, most closely translated as 'reader'—could change according to who drew them. If you were pure of heart, they would change to a spring or a White Dragon tile. If courageous and brave, a summer or Red Dragon tile. If wise, a fall or Green Dragon tile. If not . . . "

Mr. Trung gazed thoughtfully down at the blank

tile lying in his palm. "If a person lacked these things and was instead ruled by fear, the blank tiles could instantly change into Downfall tiles—ones marked with signs for Pestilence, Downfall, or Misfortune. Drawing one of these tiles forces you to return all your tiles back into the pile. Then you must start again."

He looked back up at us, his gaze somber, eyes intensely black and probing. "Of course, if your soul is plagued by deeper, blacker things—cowardice, jealousy, envy, greed, hate, or evil—the blank tiles could summon any of the Four Sacred Beasts or even worse, Chiao, ending the game and exacting the Price."

Silence.

I glanced sidelong at Kevin and saw something in his eyes, a strange longing of some kind, an aching need I'd never seen there before. For a moment, Kevin wasn't just the affable, easy-going basketball jock who liked to read. He looked much older, suddenly. Almost like my dad. "Could I hold the blank tile? See what it . . . says about me?"

Mr. Trung smiled. Once again he was just the nice old man who grew the best blueberries around. He held out the tile and dropped it into Kevin's outstretched hand. "As I said, these stories are legends, the tiles nothing more than interesting items for a curio cabinet or knick-knack shelf."

I glanced at Jake.

Still silent, he now glared at Mr. Trung with an expression of hateful rage I'd never seen before, every inch of his face screaming *liar*.

Next to me, however, Kevin was turning the smooth, blank white tile over in his fingers. "How much is it? I've only got a couple of bucks . . . "

Mr. Trung bowed his head, exuding an air of regret. "Alas, someone gave me a down payment for it this morning. But you are wise, Master Kevin, for wishing to purchase it. You are an honorable young man, one worthy of owning the Sốphận."

Kevin nodded, frowning slightly as he continued to work the blank tiles with his fingers. "Right. Okay. Yeah, I figured. It looks pretty expensive. Stupid question, but you don't have anything else like it . . . ?"

A regretful headshake. "I do not, I'm afraid. But if you're interested in any of these other items . . . ?"

The spell faded. Kevin returned the blank tile to Mr. Trung. We glanced over a few other items (Jake standing silent through it all), but eventually we said our goodbyes, nodding to Mr. Trung as we moved on.

As we left, Jake in the lead and scurrying away, I looked back, maybe for one more glimpse of that black box and its strangely exotic white ivory tiles. But I saw something else, something far more disturbing, an image that has stayed with me since that day.

Mr. Trung, standing behind his table, holding the box open before him, its white tiles gleaming in the sun. There's no way I can be certain of this, but I could've sworn he had the box pointed at Jake. It seemed as if Mr. Trung was ignoring Kevin and me, focusing entirely on Jake's quickly receding back.

And though at the time I figured I was seeing things, I thought for sure Mr. Trung was talking, murmuring, maybe even quietly chanting something, and not to himself.

But to the box and its tiles.

FOUR

SOMETHING ELSE JAKE excelled at was ferreting out deep water holes hidden underneath the creek's banks and catching what my dad called 'bottom feeders' (carp and suckerfish) by *hand*.

I kid you not. Jake would scout out spots along the creek where the bank hung out over the water, lie down and literally reach under the bank into recessed, watery alcoves. He'd then grab either a carp or a suckerfish by the gills and drag it flopping to shore.

According to my dad carp and suckers don't taste so great. But they're big, sometimes the size of large walleyes or small northern pikes. They provide plenty of *meat*, regardless of taste. Given the needs of Jake's family, taste probably wasn't a big concern. Any type of free food helped.

My dad had never taken up fishing by hand because he could never get over the fear that maybe something *else* waited for him under that bank. Like water moccasins or a snapping turtle. Jake, however, showed no fear. I suppose needing to eat and always being on guard for your father's routine unemployment served as a big motivator.

But that afternoon Jake came up strangely empty fishing for bottom feeders. We all caught some trout. I landed four, Gary five and Kevin a whopping three (I think he just liked walking in the woods more than anything else). Jake, as usual, had landed seven trout, knowing exactly where to cast his bait, as always.

Try as he might, though, he couldn't land any suckers or carp. After several bottom-feeders squirmed from his grasp, Jake finally rolled over and punched the ground, enraged. "Fuck this shit," he snarled.

I glanced at him, feeling that odd worry again. Jake hadn't been the same since the Commons Yard Sale and Mr. Trung. He'd offered one or two of his usual dirty jokes but they'd fallen flat. He hadn't ridiculed any of us when we'd gotten snagged or lost the inevitable hook or two. He'd acted quiet and withdrawn, moody and tense. Now, however, I sensed a seething anger lying beneath the surface, threatening to break out and spill everywhere.

And that's when Gary opened his big mouth.

"I dunno," Gary sniped from where he was leaning against an Adirondack pine. "Maybe you're just goin' pussy, Jake. Maybe Mr. Trung spooked ya this mornin'."

Though an obvious comeback to Jake's 'naked mom' joke, I winced and glanced at Kevin. He returned my look, eyebrows raised, and I realized he'd *also* noticed Jake's strange reaction to Mr. Trung. I saw it in his eyes, the same thing I'd felt while standing at Mr. Trung"s table: unexpected concern for Jake.

Jake scowled at us, eyes narrowed, nostrils flaring, like he wanted to kick all our asses right then and there.

"Blow me, McNamara. Ain't spooked by nobody. Specially not a fuckin gook like Mr. Hong Kong Fooey."

"I dunno, man. You looked pretty messed-up when he was showin' off that cool domino game of his. Didn't say a word an' kept starin' at your big feet the entire time. What's up with *that*?"

In a flurry of leaves, twigs and browned pine needles, Jake scrambled to his feet, hands clenched into fists. "What th'hell," he rasped between clenched teeth. "You spyi'n on me, Macky? Huh?"

Gary shrugged, looking immensely pleased with Jake's reaction. "Naw, I was just headin' back to see if you guys were ready to go an' I turned the corner an there you were, starin' at the ground, shiverin' like a scared little girl. Had to watch for a couple minutes. It was fuckin' priceless, dude."

Gary was *clearly* still pissed about Jake's taunt earlier, and tension had always simmered between them, even on a good day. But Gary's jab seemed over-the-top, completely unexpected . . .

But never in a million years could I have anticipated Jake's response. He bellowed and charged, slamming his shoulder into Gary's gut, tackling him.

Kevin and I intervened, pulling them apart, but not before they rolled and kicked and exchanged a flurry of punches that mostly glanced off each other. By the time Kevin and I got them to their feet, however— Kevin holding Jake back, me pushing Gary away—I noticed a dangerous gleam in Gary's eye that I'd never seen before. Had Jake finally crossed a line?

Gary spat on his hand. I hissed in surprise at the bloody splotch of saliva. Apparently one of Jake's flailing blows had landed after all.

Pushing and trying to shove me aside, Gary snarled, "I'm gonna fuckin' kill you, Burns."

"C'mon! You call *me* pussy? I'll show who the fuckin pussy is . . . "

"Cool it, Jake!"

Jake lurched forward against Kevin, jabbing a finger at Gary. His red face twisted into an ugly sneer. "I ain't afraid of nobody, Macky! *Nobody!*" Spittle flew and the cords in his neck stood out as he screamed. "An' I ain't afraid of that stupid Gook's goddamn fortune tellin' game! Fuck him an' his game!"

An oppressive silence fell over everything then, sharp tension building like a static charge between us. Kevin took a deep breath and broke the silence with, "Jake. What the *hell* is wrong? You can tell us, man. It's okay."

I'm ashamed to confess how I felt just then. Here was this kid who really annoyed the piss out of us (me especially), dogging our steps every day; a kid with *issues*; a kid whose presence offered very few perks, and here Kevin was trying to make peace with him while I just wanted Jake to storm off into the woods and leave us alone.

I got my wish. Jake glared at Gary for several seconds, face red and teeth bared like a dog. Then he hissed, "Fuck y'all. I don't need your help, or your shit."

He shook himself free of Kevin's grip and stalked away, stooping to grab his line of fish from the water in one hand and his pole in the other. He slouched toward Black Creek Bridge and Clarke Street, leaving us in the woods staring at each other, leaving me to wonder just what it was about Mr. Trung that scared Jake Burns so much.

SOPHAN

I'd find out soon enough.
Though I still wish I hadn't.

FIVE

I T NAGGED ME on my ride home after we all parted ways on Asher Street: something was *wrong* with Jake. Something had *always* been wrong with him. It wasn't just how annoying he was or his lack of social graces or his dirty jokes that weren't funny or even his lightning-quick temper. It lay deeper, and somehow I understood without actually knowing it had something to do with his dad. Which made me think about the similarities between Jake's dad and mine, and how similar we were, in a way . . . even if I didn't want to admit it.

Neither of us had a mom. Both our dads worked at the lumber mill (until Jake's got fired a few months ago) and both fought in Vietnam. Even though he wasn't a drunk like Jake's dad, my dad liked a beer every day after work to wind down.

This also made me think even more about how Jake had latched onto me, following *me* around the most. In a burst of juvenile paranoia, I started worrying that maybe Jake hung around me so much because he *recognized* something *in* me that he connected to, that maybe, someday, given the right factors . . . I'd be like Jake, even.

SOPHAN

It was ridiculous.

But it went a long way (in my fevered little brain, anyway) toward explaining why Jake had pegged me for his best friend. By the time I skidded to a dusty stop in our gravel driveway I was stewing over it so bad I couldn't think of anything else. Actually, I didn't think of much else for the next few days, though I hid it well, as always.

Just like I've hidden it for the past twenty years.

SIX

T HID MY worries for two days. After we'd finished dinner Tuesday night and I'd washed the dishes, Dad was relaxing in the den watching the Mets with his nightly post-dinner beer. I worked up the nerve to poke my head around the corner. "Dad . . . got a minute?"

Dad always listened to me, taking everything I said seriously, never treating me like a kid. Even if the Yankees were playing the Mets at Shea Stadium and it was the bottom of the ninth, he'd block it out and listen. I'll always be grateful for that.

Which makes me feel even worse about how I've turned out.

Anyway he stood, walked to the television and shut it off, sat back down and raised an eyebrow. "What's up?"

"I won't end up like Jake Burns someday, will I? And you won't ever be like his dad . . . will you?"

Dad sat forward, frowning slightly. "What brings *this* on? You guys aren't havin' any troubles with Jake, are you? I mean, any more'n usual." He paused, eyes narrowing. "His dad isn't . . . "

I shook my head. "Nope, nothing like that.

42

Something happened Saturday and he got mad at us, and well . . . something's wrong with Jake, isn't there? And his dad."

Dad sat back and sighed, lifted his beer, thought better of it and lowered it, looking out the den window. His frown disappeared. He looked regretful, like maybe he felt bad about something that wasn't his fault, even though he felt partly responsible for it.

He chewed his lip, and then finally said, gazing out the den window into our front yard, "Yeah. I suppose somethin' is wrong with Jake and his dad." He looked back to me. "But why are you suddenly so worried we'll end up the same way?"

I shrugged, my concerns seeming weak in the light of day. "Well . . . I mean, our moms are both gone. You and Jake's dad both fought in Vietnam and . . . "

I stopped short, unable to bring up Dad's nightly beer. He'd never once gotten drunk that I'd known, and I thought that might be going too far.

Dad smiled and waved at the rocking chair next to him, the one he said had always been Mom's favorite before she died. "Sit, Nate. Let's talk."

I took a seat. He leaned back, sighed again, then looked me in the eye. "You're right about some things. Both me and Jimmy Burns fought in Vietnam. Both of us lost our wives, leavin' you and Jake without moms. And, though you didn't say it, maybe you're thinkin' it: Jake's dad loves his drink, and I have a beer after dinner every night. But I'm not Jimmy, and you'll never end up like Jake, Nate. I promise."

I squirmed a little in the rocking chair. I wanted to believe Dad but couldn't shake my worry. "How d'you know, Dad? Really."

"Well for one, Jake probably feels abandoned by his mom and you don't. Jake's momma up and *left*. Probably 'cause she couldn't handle Jimmy anymore. And she *didn't* take Jake with her, or even say goodbye. Now, knowin' 'em like I do I figure that's cause she was afraid of tryin' to take Jake away from Jimmy. But I'm sure Jake don't know that, and he probably thinks his mom ditched him. Your mom was *taken* from us, Nate. She woulda moved heaven'n earth to stay, and . . . "

He coughed, rubbed the corner of his eye with the palm of his hand, cleared his throat and continued, "And I think even if you don't know that consciously, some parta ya understands that, deep down. Also, I think a big reason why somethin's wrong with Jake is cause somethin's wrong with Jimmy, *bad*."

I frowned because this I didn't understand too well, how Jake's dad and my dad could be so different. "What's wrong with him? Is it because of Vietnam? And why . . . "

"Why ain't there nothin' wrong with me?" Dad offered me a sad-looking grin then, maybe the saddest I'd ever seen from him. "I ain't gonna lie, son. I got my scars. Still have powerful bad dreams every now and then. And if it weren't for your mom, the way she took care of me when I got home . . . well. It was hard on *every* man who fought over there. I pray you never hafta serve. Me and my unit got off lucky, though. We saw some hard fightin' and I saw good friends die. But other platoons got caught up in some bad business and did some bad things. Sometimes you're fightin' so hard to live you forget who you are and what you're fightin' for. Lotta men went through that kinda bad business, and I'm blessed to have been spared it."

44

"Is that what happened to Jake's dad?"

Dad's smile faded entirely. He rubbed his mouth and said, "No. Worse. Y'know how you're always sayin' Jake's so good at findin' them fish, knowin' where they're hidin'?"

I nodded.

"Well, Jimmy was like that, too. Bout the time he was old 'nough to hunt he could sneak round like a mountain cat, like a native Algonquin. Bow, rifle . . . he could hunt just 'bout anythin' and he drifted like a ghost through the woods, too. We both did Basic Training down in Camp Dix for regular Army, but wasn't long before folks picked up on Jimmy's gift and picked him for the Green Berets."

A memory sparked of a movie I'd seen during a Sunday afternoon matinee on television. "Wasn't there a John Wayne movie with Green Berets in it? They wore these funny little hats instead of helmets?"

He smiled a little sadly again. "Yeah, but it wasn't like the movies, son. Them Green Berets in real life? Hell."

He sat back in his chair and took a swig of beer, while I sat in mildly stunned silence. I knew my dad swore occasionally—all adults did—but he'd always been careful about swearing around me before. That he'd say "hell" so casually and not apologize for it shocked me.

He set his beer down and wiped his mouth again. "They were hard fellas, Nate. Machines. I'd like to think us regular Army boys were pretty tough. I held my own, and I knew plenty fellas in my platoon that were braver'n tougher'n crazier'n me. Those Green Berets, though . . . I'm not even sure they was human by the time they pulled us outta there. Fact, I heard plenty stories 'bout how bunches of 'em slipped off into the jungle when the final orders came to pull out, and no one ever saw nor heard from 'em again."

"What was wrong with them, Dad. Were they . . . bad?"

Dad looked sad again. "A few, maybe. But most were regular folks. Here's the difference: in the regular Army, they train you to defend yourself and kill if you hafta. I killed some men, son. Didn't want to, and I still have some bad dreams now and again . . . but it was them or me, straight shootin', and in the end I'm glad it was them, and I don't feel too bad about it at all."

"But the Green Berets?"

"They weren't trained just to defend themselves. They was trained to *kill*. Whether or not anyone was tryin' to kill them. They was taught how to sneak in the night and kill men in their beds, kill women and kids, too, if they got in the way. And the military ain't like school, Nate. You either stayed and did everythin' their way, or you got sent home in disgrace, and that was just *regular* Army. Once you went deep as the Green Berets, there was no choices no more. Not even to go home."

"So . . . they changed him," I whispered, feeling a deep sense of a sadness I didn't understand. "Changed him and made him . . . different."

"Yes, that's 'bout right. Not gonna lie, the war changed all of us, turned hundreds of young men into scarred men overnight. But them Green Berets . . . they got changed by their own people, and lots of 'em couldn't never change back."

"Like Jimmy."

46

He nodded. "Yes, like Jimmy."

"If he got changed so bad, why're you still friends? Why keep getting him re-hired every time he gets fired, why do you . . . "

"Still spend time with him?" Dad shrugged. "This'll probably sound strange, but when he's sober and we're out in the woods huntin' or fishin', he's a lot like his old self. Older of course and scarred like me, but more like he used to be. And . . . I suppose in a weird way I feel guilty. I came back and had a tough time but I had yer mom, and . . . well, I *made* it. Was able to live a normal life again. As normal as any of us ever live, anyway. But my *buddy* . . . like you and Kevin are buddies . . . didn't make it back. He left something' important over there'n that jungle, and he ain't never gonna get it back. I suppose I feel bad about that."

"He . . . he hits Jake, I think." My voice rasped and my throat stung. I wanted to cry but couldn't. "Hits him and . . . maybe does worse stuff."

Dad nodded very slowly, suddenly looking tired and old. "I know, son. I've tried hundreds of times to work myself up to say somethin' to him or someone else . . . but I'm afraid it'll just make things worse for Jake, and to have a hand in takin' a man's children away, when that man ain't got nothin' else . . . well, that's a hard thing, Nate. A hard thing."

We lapsed into silence. The clock ticked against the quiet. Finally, Dad roused himself and took a deep breath. "The world is a hard place, Nate. Bad things happen to lots of folks. I'm sure as the sun rises you'll weather your share of troubles. But you're not Jake and I'm not Jimmy. You don't have to worry about those things happenin' to us."

I smiled and meant it, though a small cold knot of unease still coiled in my stomach. "Thanks, Dad. A bunch."

He nodded, and though I didn't really like baseball, I watched the rest of the game with Dad in a companionable silence for the remainder of the evening.

❧

Dad was right about how he'd never turn bad, like Jake's dad.

Unfortunately, he wasn't so right about me.

SEVEN

DESPITE DAD'S REASSURANCES that night, I had a nightmare, one of the worst I'd ever had. We were all back at the Commons Yard Sale—me, Kevin and Jake—standing before Mr. Trung's table. I couldn't move, frozen in that way we usually are in nightmares. The air felt thick and humid. Everything sounded muffled, as if we stood underwater.

Chanting guttural words, Mr. Trung laid tiles out in overlapping rows. I couldn't see the engravings on them because they blurred and moved across the ivory. He laid the tiles, arranging them, preparing them . . .

For us to play.

Then Mr. Trung stopped his strange, gurgling song. He stared at each of us in turn. I desperately tried to move my arms, legs, head, *something*, but I couldn't. I was locked in place, joints frozen, feet rooted to the ground. Mr. Trung's eyes—much larger and a deeper black than I'd ever seen—seemed to peel back layers of me until I felt raw, exposed and quivering beneath his gaze.

Mr. Trung reached into the black wooden box and withdrew a single white tile. Turning his gaze to Kevin, he held it up at an angle that wouldn't allow me to see it. Then, he laid it before Kevin on the table and nodded. Though I couldn't move and my gaze remained fixed on Mr. Trung's face, I felt a *releasing*. Kevin had been freed.

Mr. Trung did the same with me. He reached into the box, withdrew a tile and held it up. The tile's engraving twisted, turned and shivered. I thought I saw . . . something.

A red dragon.

Or maybe white.

I couldn't tell. But I felt a sudden, overwhelming sense of freedom. When Mr. Trung nodded and laid the tile before me as he'd done with Kevin, my limbs fell loose and free. I knew that not only could I leave . . .

I had to.

Even if it meant leaving Jake behind.

The worst thing about the nightmare was not what happened to me, it was what I did . . . exactly that. I turned from Mr. Trung and walked away from that table, following Kevin's receding form, leaving Jake to face his tile alone.

And when Jake's shrill screams filled the air, I bolted awake, tangled bed sheets sticking to me, my heart thundering in my chest.

I didn't sleep much the rest of the night.

EIGHT

I DIDN'T REALIZE until breakfast when my sister Amy asked what I'd done with the blueberries that I'd forgotten to stop by Mr. Trung's on the way home from fishing Saturday. Dad had already left for work so Amy felt the freedom to call me several choice names, questioning the number of chromosomes I'd been born with. I basically told her to "shove it."

But I knew how much Dad loved blueberry pie. Eager to keep him in a good mood so I could attend that night's showing of *The Creature from the Black Lagoon* at Raedeker Park, I finally told Amy very kindly to "shut your cake-hole, I'll get the damned blueberries." She then threatened to tell Dad I'd said "damned." I countered with a threat to tell Dad about the older boy she'd been dating on the sly from Webb County Community College (Amy was only a junior in high school). That pretty much sealed everything up in a tense truce, so I left the house that morning feeling pretty *damned* productive, indeed.

So damned productive that it wasn't until about a quarter of a mile away from Mr. Trung's that I remembered my nightmare from last night, remembered how I'd left Jake standing there alone to face Mr. Trung and that gleaming ivory tile; left him alone . . .

And screaming.

It was too late to back out, however. Amy pissed me off sometimes (being the general pain in the ass all older sisters are) but we'd made a deal. It wasn't like I had anything else better to do. It was Wednesday morning. Kevin would be chopping firewood for his dad. Gary would be working concessions at Raedeker Park. I was pretty much on my own until about ten, when I had to bale hay at the Drake's, so off to Mr. Trung's it was.

Half an hour later, however, I skidded my bike to a stop at Mr. Trung's driveway, halted by a "Closed" sign hanging from the wooden gate leading to his blueberry patch.

And that was odd.

Because Mr. Trung hardly ever closed his blueberry patch.

He did sometimes leave up a "Help Yourself" sign. When that happened, you grabbed a few pint containers from the small shed sitting next to the gate, picked what you wanted, weighed out on the scales in back of the shed, then slipped your cash or even an IOU into a locked cash box. Pretty much everyone played straight with Mr. Trung. I suppose one or two local kids occasionally took advantage of the old man's trust, snagging some free berries, but he never mentioned it and it never seemed to hurt business.

But *closed*?

Almost unheard of.

At first I felt oddly relieved. Mr. Trung wasn't around. He'd closed for some reason, so I couldn't pick blueberries. But then I remembered the deal I'd made with Amy. If I welched I'd never hear the end of it.

So with a few misgivings I said, "Screw it." I parked my bike, grabbed a pint container from the shed and spent the next hour picking blueberries. I drifted from bush to bush, not really thinking, just enjoying the quiet. Memories of my nightmare and my worries about turning out like Jake faded. I felt content to just pick blueberries and be alone for a while.

And then I heard it.

Soft whispering on the warm, still air.

Singing.

Chanting, like Mr. Trung's gurgling song from my nightmare. It was coming from nearby, from his carefully manicured flower garden on the other side of his trailer.

As popular as his blueberry patch was, his flower garden and koi pond were the talk of the town. Meticulously sculptured, his flower garden consisted of snap-dragons, posies, tulips, roses, lilies, and Black Eyed-Susans. The most impressive feature was the koi pond and the Oriental-style gazebo in the garden's center.

The pond was rectangular, bordered by a smaller hedge and adorned with beautiful, blooming white water lilies. At one end stone steps led down into the pool, which was a much speculated affectation. Why would anyone build stone steps leading into an ornamental pond in a flower garden?

That day I learned the answer. The blueberry patch sat on a slight rise above the flower garden and koi

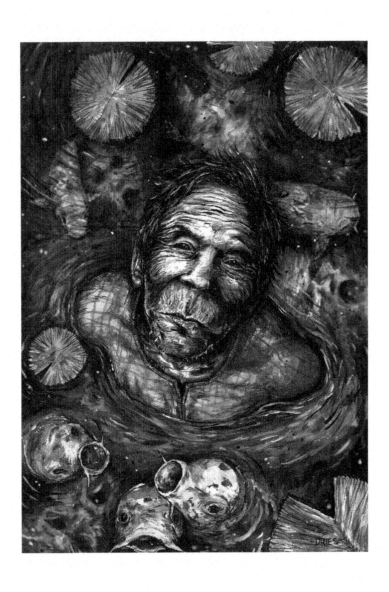

pond. I could see the pond clearly. As I watched, dumbfounded, amazed and maybe even a little frightened, I saw Mr. Trung (dressed in white robes) slowly descend those steps into the koi pond. Though it strained believability, he kept going until his head disappeared under the water completely. His sighing chant faded into silence.

I stood and stared for at least ten or fifteen minutes, during which I didn't see even a *ripple* across the pond. After five more minutes, however, Mr. Trung rose to the surface. And I don't mean walked back up the steps again. I mean *rose*. As in levitated. He floated up from the water, to his waist. He spread his arms, looked up into the sky . . . and began chanting again.

And the fish.

The Koi.

All puckering in the water around Mr. Trung.

I stood frozen, afraid to keep looking but afraid to move, thinking of that "Closed" sign and sensing that if Mr. Trung discovered me he would not be the kindly old man I'd always known. Something whispered in me that others weren't supposed to see this, that it was private, hence the "Closed" sign.

But he never noticed me. Or, if he knew I was watching, he never let on. The puckering slowed and stopped. Dim yellow and orange flashes swam away from Mr. Trung, back into the pond's depths. He turned his face to the sky once more, brought his hands together as if in prayer, then slowly moved up the steps, out of the pond and back toward his trailer, out of sight.

I'm not sure how much longer I stood there, but eventually it hit me: What if Mr. Trung came out *right now* and saw my bike? How could I explain my presence, especially with that "Closed" sign hanging on the gate?

So I finished picking with rare abandon, filling both pint containers quickly, then stuffed a few bucks into the shed's cash box on my way out. As luck would have it, when I finally got back on my bike Mr. Trung was still nowhere to be found. However, I couldn't shake the feeling something was watching me. Even worse, I felt that thing was in the Koi pond, which was ridiculous. How could fish be watching me?

Stupid.

Even so, it wasn't until I'd biked several miles down the road that the uneasy chill left my neck and shoulders.

NINE

AFTER DROPPING THE blueberries off at home (and telling myself over and over that Mr. Trung hadn't seen me hiding in his bushes) I pedaled to Bobby Drake's farm to bale hay. Bobby's dad ran a dairy farm just outside town. That's where most of us earned our cash. It was pretty much an all-summer occupation. With Kevin still most likely chopping firewood it was just me and Bobby and Bobby's younger brother Matt . . . and, well, the last person I expected to see: Jake. Of course, Jake's family needed the money—his dad out of work again—and Mr. Drake always welcomed the extra help.

We all arrived in front of the Drake barn around ten. Mr. Drake pulled his tractor out, hitched up one of his wagons. We clambered on and trundled off. We usually worked until we filled that wagon, then afterward we'd hitch up an empty wagon, work straight until noon and break for lunch, which Mrs. Drake always packed into a cooler for us.

Then we'd get back to work. Once we filled the wagons, we'd return to Drake's barn to load the hayloft. Mr. Drake "officially" let helpers go by four in the afternoon because by then our parents were expecting us for dinner. Bobby and his dad, however, sometimes worked until sundown.

That day seemed like a regular day. At first I felt uneasy seeing Jake so soon after what happened Saturday in the woods. But it wasn't long before we fell into the usual rhythms of baling hay and those weird memories faded.

Bobby, the most experienced, worked the back of the wagon stacking. Jake and I snagged bales thrown by the kicker, passing them to Bobby. Bobby's little brother Matt "trailed," which basically meant he followed the wagon on foot, tracking down errant bales, collecting and dragging them to a smaller flat-bed trailer at the field's edge. In some ways it was probably an easier job than working the wagon. If things worked out right, Matt just walked behind us the whole time. Personally, I preferred working the wagon. Constantly catching and handing bales off to Bobby passed the time more quickly than following the wagon by foot.

That's how the morning passed into the afternoon. Though it may seem weird to anyone who didn't grow up in the country, I felt a pleasant sense of industry. Working and *doing* something, stacking the wagon and then filling the hayloft filled a very basic need. Also, four bucks an hour didn't hurt, either.

We fell into a pleasant routine. I'd hear the whine-*chunk* of the kicker, grab a bale and pass it to Bobby. I'd hear that whine-*chunk* again, knowing Jake would grab that one and pass it while I waited to catch the next. When the wagon got nearly full, leaving us perched on the end, Mr. Drake turned the kicker off. We headed over to the flat-bed full of loose bales to fill in the holes before switching to an empty wagon and starting the whole process over.

By the time lunch rolled around I'd almost forgotten about Mr. Trung and Jake. Amazingly, Jake had acted tolerable. No stupid dirty jokes and no petulance. He didn't even rag me for moving too slow (which he often did, because he was Jake and that's what he did). That morning he worked hard, kept quiet, and several times I almost forgot he was there.

Then came lunch. Bobby, Jake and I sat in an empty wagon eating our sandwiches. Matt had run home for lunch because he'd wanted ice cream. Mr. Drake was enjoying his lunch and maybe a cold beer on the tractor.

We were busily chewing our sandwiches when Bobby asked, "You hitting the movie tonight? Think it's a monster flick. Creature from the Black Lagoon."

I swallowed and nodded. "Absolutely. Last week's movie was Little Orphan Annie. So lame. Gonna meet up with Bill Ward. He loves those old monster movies."

Bobby smiled. "Funny. Pastor's Kid into horror movies. But he's pretty solid. Not like some PKs."

"Yeah, he's cool. Got a nice comic book collection, too."

Then I did it. I still don't know why, because until that moment Jake had eaten quietly, staring off over the field. There had been no reason to include him in the conversation. Over the years I've played that moment over in my head, wondering if things would've turned out differently if I'd just kept on ignoring Jake.

However, relaxed by the bright sun and sweat on

my shoulders, I turned to Jake and asked, "You going to the movie tonight? You liked the last monster movie they played."

Jake took a bite of his sandwich and chewed slowly. A grin blossomed. He swallowed and before he took another bite he said, "Naw. Got somethin *way* better planned than a dumb-ass movie."

Bobby sighed. He'd heard that before. Everyone had. It was Jake's usual precursor to whatever crazy-ass scheme he'd cooked up. "Let me guess. It involves fire-crackers and lighting a bag of dog crap on Mrs. Wilkins' back porch."

Jake shook his head. Took a bite, chewed and swallowed and said, "Naw, not this time." Crazy thing was, he meant it when he said 'not *this* time.' That was Jake for you.

"Naw, I gotta a better idea. Somethin' special planned for that gook bastard Mr. Trung. Fuckin slant-eye. Teach him a lesson, tryin' to embarrass me an' shit."

Bobby and I exchanged a worried glance. He also looked confused, having had no idea what had happened at the Commons Yard Sale. I turned and frowned at Jake, a cold knot forming in my gut. "What are you going to do?"

Jake didn't answer. He just sat there and grinned. I repeated my question a bit more forcefully. "Jake! What are you gonna do?"

Jake looked at me straight in the eyes. I saw something flash there. His eyes glittered but they also looked flat, dead and *gone*.

"I'm gonna fix that gook bastard," he said slowly. "I'm gonna fix his ass. Teach him a lesson about fuckin' with me *or* my dad."

SOPHAN

He finished his sandwich. Wiped his hands on his pants. Stood, and without another word jumped down from the wagon, circled around its back and disappeared into the woods. He just walked off and didn't bother collecting his pay, even though I knew he and his family needed the money.

That moment stands out in my mind and bothers me the most. Jake, striking off like that without collecting the money we all knew he and his family needed so much. It was like he'd known, even then, what was going to happen.

He'd known and had given up caring.

TEN

I MET BILL Ward at Raedeker Park around seven. *The Creature from the Black Lagoon* started at eight, so we bought some hotdogs from the concession stand and walked through the zoo, because they always offered free admission an hour before the weekly movie. Raedeker Recreational Park wasn't just an athletic field and a playground. It was a collection of various attractions on the west end of town. Down Barstow Road past the New York State Electric and Gas Payment Center, left onto Samara Hill and about two miles up on the right sprawled Raedeker Recreational Park. Upon entering, if you went straight, you'd take a winding road descending to Raedeker Park Zoo.

The zoo wasn't that impressive. It offered only a moderate collection of animals, always permeated by a mild air of dilapidation, constantly under a renovation that never seemed to end. According to Dad, it started to go downhill years ago after it suffered a rash of weird accidents. First, a train ride derailed, resulting in minor injuries and a broken arm. A few weeks later, the carousel's engine went bonkers, spinning too fast and causing a heart attack. The *coup de grace* was a lion mauling an animal trainer to death.

Though my friends never mentioned it, I always experienced a moment of mild trepidation when riding the carousel. I wondered if it would inexplicably speed up and carry me to my death, too. The lion cage was still there, open for the public. It had become a slightly spooky ritual to go inside and pretend the ghost of the trainer or the lion still lurked about, ready to take its vengeance on those disturbing their rest.

Nothing but rusted tracks remained of the train ride, though. That one accident jacked up the Park's insurance rates too high and they had to tear it down, according to Dad.

If you take a left when you enter the park, you'll pass the requisite playground with a basketball court. In the small hollow behind it lay a surprisingly large outdoor amphitheater. Its wooden benches lined the bank and the stage sat down in the hollow. The dense Adirondack forest loomed behind. On that stage actors performed dramas for theater lovers, bands played for special events and once a week during the summer a big movie screen reared its square white head, presenting everything from creature-features to old westerns.

While Bill Ward and I sat eating hot dogs in the amphitheater, a thought occurred to me. "Hey. Can I ask a sorta . . . personal question?

Bill smiled. "Sure. What's up?"

"Your dad's a pastor and all. He knows almost everyone in Clifton Heights, right?"

"Yeah. Guess so."

"Does he know Mr. Trung?"

"The blueberry guy? Sure. What about him?"

"Well . . . I guess this is a weird question . . . but, does your dad know what . . . religion he is? I was just wondering, because I never see him in church."

If Bill thought my question odd he didn't let on. He just shrugged. "My dad'n him are on the Town Board. They talk a lot, but he's never mentioned it. Maybe Mr. Trung is Buddhist or something? Lots of Vietnamese are."

"What do Buddhists believe?"

"Reincarnation and karma. Stuff like that. What we do in this life affects our next life and what happens to us now is *because* of what we did in our past life, and that we go up and down depending on how we live in each life."

A light flicked on in my head. At the beginning of the school year in World History we learned that reincarnation meant coming back to life as an animal, or that maybe you were an animal before and the second time around you came back as a human . . .

Mr. Trung praying in his koi pond and the fish praying to him.

. . . and if you did good things you got the good things you deserved and if you did bad things . . .

Like Jake's dad in Vietnam.

. . . you got the bad things you deserved.

I looked away from Bill, stunned by this strange revelation. "Wow," I breathed.

Bill nodded, misunderstanding my shock as simple wonder. "Yeah. Interesting, huh? I don't know how I feel about it, but what if we have Jesus and the cross and they have that?" He shook his head, looking back at the movie screen, which was showing the old

64

fashioned countdown before the movie began. "Like I said, interesting."

I agreed.

But for very different reasons, as the image of Mr. Trung praying in his koi pond . . .

As the koi prayed to him.

. . . played over and over in my head as the movie began.

ELEVEN

I'D ALWAYS LOVED Creature from the Black Lagoon, even though I'd already seen it several times before on Channel 34's Sunday afternoon cinema. It was campy and a bit silly, overacted, and I was well old enough to know the monster was a guy in a rubber suit . . .

But despite that, something in the beginning gave me a bad turn that night. After Dr. Maia (played by Antonio Moren), discovered the petrified hand-fossil of the Creature's ancestor, the *live* Creature reached menacingly out of the Amazon's waters to scrape its claws on the bank. It was an amazingly effective shot despite the brassy musical score accompanying it. The only thing shown is that webbed claw, looking terribly life-like in black and white (to an imaginative fourteen year old, anyway), reaching out of the water and clawing the bank, almost as if it was marking its territory.

But the jolt I suffered that night had little to do with cinematography and to do more with the images conjured in my head of something similar clawing its way out of Mr. Trung's koi pond, those webbed claws scraping the stone ledge bordering the rectangular pool . . .

Even as I shook the image away, telling myself it was a stupid thought, I couldn't banish the image of Mr. Trung rising from the pool, arms outstretched, chanting softly as the koi fish puckered around him, praying to him . . .

Worshiping him.

Despite how much I'd been looking forward to that movie, I had a hard time following the rest of it. When the credits finally rolled I acted just as enthusiastic as Bill did, nodding in all the right places as he talked about what he called the "lonely monster as outsider," but really, I felt relieved the night was over.

The night wasn't over, however. I knew that the instant Jake eased his bike out of the dark alley between Chin's Pizza and Dooley's Ice Cream, after Bill and I parted ways at Allen Street. And the weirdest part?

I wasn't surprised to see him.

TWELVE

I SQUEEZED MY bike's handbrakes, slowing to a stop. "Jake," I said, feeling oddly calm, for some reason. "What's up?"

He shrugged, his face weirdly blank in the yellow glow of the streetlights.

"Were you at the movie? Didn't see you."

He shook his head. "Nah. I . . . uh, had some thinkin' to do. About stuff. Hey," he leaned over his handlebars, face finally coming alive, looking eager, nervous, maybe excited . . . and . . .

Yes.

Afraid.

"Listen. I'm gonna do somethin' tonight. I need help. Someone to watch out. Could . . . could you go with me? I'm sorry for the way I freaked out in the woods Saturday. I just . . . I need your help, man. Need you to watch out for me."

I stared at him: his brow furrowed, jaw firm, a vein pulsing on his temple, eyes wide and glimmering. I knew where he wanted to go but I asked anyway. "Where?"

And then I saw it, creeping back into his face as a gradual sneer—that old Jake Burns look, but with something else burning his eyes.

SOPHAN

Hate.

Absolute hate. And I wondered for the first time what *exactly* Jake's dad had done to him. The man who'd gone to Vietnam, joined the Green Berets, done 'bad things' and returned home broken.

"We're goin' to Mr. Trung's place. That gook bastard. I'm gonna fuckin' take back what he took from my old man."

I sat back on my bike, surprise rippling through me, because Jake's answer was and wasn't what I'd been expecting. Given Jake's transformation over the past few days since we'd run into Mr. Trung at the Commons Yard Sale, I'd expected he'd want to do something stupid, like go back and either mess with Mr. Trung's blueberries or even worse, go after the fish in his koi pond . . .

Where Mr. Trung was praying.

And the koi were praying to him.

. . . but something hotter than vandalism burned in Jake's eyes. He wanted revenge. He meant it when he said Mr. Trung had taken something from his dad. Sitting in the glow of the streetlights, I thought of the way Mr. Trung had stared at Jake the other day. Somehow, I knew.

Jake was telling the truth.

Mr. Trung *had* taken something from his father. He meant to get it back. But . . .

"What? Get back what, Jake?"

"His soul, dammit. Fuckin gook took my dad's soul, and I'm fuckin gettin' it back.

"Tonight."

THIRTEEN

I 'M STILL NOT sure why I followed Jake out to Mr. Trung's. Dad had set pretty firm rules for the night. I could go to the weekly movie on my bike alone, so long as I returned home by eleven, allowing for some dawdling after the movie and the ride home. But here I was, flying down Bassler Road behind Jake Burns at what had to be eleven already.

Usually Dad went to bed before us because he had to report to the lumber mill by five, but who knew? Maybe he wouldn't be able to sleep. Maybe he'd wait up and when I didn't come home like I was supposed to he'd wait up some more, come out looking for me or call the sheriff, even. Worse, maybe Amy had come home early, noticed my absence and in true big-sister fashion, ratted me out. Could be either of those fates was in store.

Or maybe neither of them. Maybe Dad had gone to bed as usual—around 8:00, right after his nightly beer—and had fallen hard asleep like always. Maybe Amy was still out with her friends and wouldn't get home until 12, which was her summer curfew, being a junior and all.

But it didn't matter. Something I couldn't define

had formed a strange bond between Jake and I. He rode through the night, his tires humming and his bike chain buzzing to the peepers keening in the woods and I followed, connected to Jake by an invisible, indestructible tether.

He had asked for help.

My help.

The entire time we'd known Jake he'd followed us around, trying desperately to be one of us and failing miserably, but he'd never once asked us for anything.

And he'd asked *me* for help.

Me.

To help get his father's soul back from Mr. Trung.

I had no idea what that meant, but as I followed Jake down Bassler Road I knew I had to follow him all the way to the end. If I'd known that would be the last time I'd ever see him?

I wouldn't have acted any differently.

FOURTEEN

J AKE BROUGHT HIS bike to a skidding stop along Bassler Road's gravel shoulder. I followed suit. We walked our bikes the rest of the way. As we turned onto Mr. Trung's property, his trailer leaped from the darkness, a dim white ghost partially lit by one porch light.

To our left the rows of blueberry bushes looked like dark, impenetrable walls of a maze. On the other side of the trailer lay Mr. Trung's beautifully manicured flower gardens and his koi pond . . .

Mr. Trung, praying in the koi pond.

The koi praying to him.

. . . and I felt a surge of inexplicable relief that Mr. Trung's trailer blocked my view of the garden and that koi pond.

The koi.

Praying to Mr. Trung.

"Here," Jake whispered as he cut off the road, across the shallow ditch and along the edge of Mr. Trung's property. "Quieter than the driveway."

I followed him—still tugged along by some strange insistence I didn't understand—looking at Mr. Trung's darkened trailer. No lights shone in the windows. Only the one porch light cast a pale-white spill on the small little porch and the surrounding ground. I noticed the empty driveway and whispered, "Where's Mr. Trung?"

"Dunno," Jake whispered back over his shoulder. "He goes somewhere every Wednesday night. Maybe some weird gook church or somethin'. He won't be back until around midnight or so."

In the dark I wheeled my bike over a fallen tree branch. The cracking-*snap* broke the silence like a barking Daisy rifle. We froze for several seconds, petrified, staring at Mr. Trung's dark home. When nothing stirred and we heard only the chirping peepers, I hunched over my bike's handlebars and rasped, "Howdya know for sure he won't be back soon?"

Jake glanced at me, managing to look sly despite the scare we'd just had. "Every Wednesday he leaves 'round six and don't come back until after midnight."

A chill that had nothing to do with the night crept up the back of my neck, thinking about Jake crouched here in the woods night after night, watching Mr. Trung's place. "How long you been coming here at night?"

That simmering look of hate returned, large eyes glimmering in the dark. "A few months. Ever since . . . it happened."

"What? *What* happened? What are we doing here? Tell me right now Jake, or I'm bailing. I'm late enough to get my ass whipped as it is and if we get caught out here or if someone calls the Sheriff . . . "

"All right, all right!" He snapped at me. "Don't be such a pussy! Here," he nodded at the very first row of blueberry bushes, only a few feet away. We wheeled ourselves over, thankfully avoiding any more fallen branches, pulled our bikes into the row and crouched there, effectively hidden.

"What the hell's going on, Jake? Why are we here? What did Mr. Trung do to your dad?"

Jake didn't answer right away. He looked down and started picking at the grass, plucking up strands one right after the other. A deep silence descended over us, even the peepers fell silent, as if listening for what Jake had to say.

"Jake?"

"My dad fought in Vietnam. Didja know that?" I nodded silently as he continued. "He was a Green Beret. Killed gooks all over the place, and not just the VC but villagers and even little kids, cause you couldn't trust anyone there, Nate. Every gook wanted to get him and his buddies, dirty fuckin' gooks all over the place killin' everybody, all my dad's buddies, every single day. Old men with machine guns, kids with bombs strapped to 'em. Little girls, even. Goddamn gook bastards."

As he talked, the strange connection between us faded. I realized with a sudden clarity that Dad was right. I'd never end up quite like Jake because my dad came back from Vietnam whole. Maybe hurt real bad, his heart beat-up, but he'd made it back whole. He'd eventually healed and became the man he was today, raised me the way he had.

Vietnam had broken Jake's dad. Whatever happened to him, whatever he'd done had broken something deep inside him, and he'd passed that brokenness on to Jake. For the first time since I'd known him I no longer considered Jake an annoyance

74

to be tolerated or ignored. I felt a deep sense of profound sadness. Not only would I never turn out quite like Jake, most likely he'd never be like me or Kevin or Gary. He'd always be broken because his dad had passed that on to him. His dad had *done* that to him, and it was a wound that most likely would never heal.

"Y'know what my dad did in Vietnam?" Jake asked, still plucking at the grass, his movements becoming more agitated. "He was a tunnel rat. Gooks dug tunnels underground to smuggle weapons through and move around for ambushes. Tunnel rats squeezed down in them tunnels to suss them gooks out, or to find maps and weapons and shit. That's what Dad did, all the time, with nothin' but a .45 and a flashlight. He was good at it, too. Good at findin' them gooks hidin' in the dark down there underground, good at killin' them."

He looked up finally, black eyes glittering madly in the dark. "Gooks like that fuckin' Mr. Trung, who took my daddy's goddamn *soul*."

At first I thought Jake was talking in metaphor (though I had no idea what that word even meant back then), that Mr. Trung (representing the Vietnamese) had robbed Mr. Burns' soul in the *war*. Staring at Jake's burning black eyes I realized Jake meant Mr. Trung had *actually* stolen his dad's soul, which was really above my head. "Jake . . . what d'ya mean? How could . . . "

Jake shook his head, not really listening to me as he continued. "That Gook bastard. Thinks he's so great. Drivin' around that nice car of his, sellin' his goddamn blueberries with his shitty flower gardens and shitty fish, thinkin' he's so big an . . . "

"Jake!" I rasped as loud as I dared. "What the *hell*?"

Then I heard the most awful sound. Something I'd never heard from Jake before, ever. A wracking, gurgling *sob*. Jake was crying, holding his face in his hands, shoulders quaking.

"T-Two m-months ago. Got t-tired of it, tired of s-seein' that gook struttin' round like he was big man while my dad hurt every goddamn day cause gooks like Mr. Trung killed all his buddies." He wiped his eyes, sucked in a deep breath and rambled on. "So one day, right after school let out I said 'Fuck it, Imma fuck him up good, teach that gook a lesson to act all high'n mighty when my dad . . . my dad . . . '"

He stuttered, on the brink of crying again. He drew his knees tightly to his chest, buried his face into them and rocked slightly back and worth, muttering, "He has nightmares alla time and he can't sleep so he's gotta drink so he'll pass out and sleep but sometimes he don't do that, sometimes he goes after me and Emma, and . . . "

I swallowed down a sour taste, sickened by the thought of Mr. Burns turning on Jake and his ten-year-old sister, Emma. "It's all them gooks' fault," Jake rasped into his knees. "All them gooks' fault for makin' him this way, makin' him so scared and angry alla time . . . "

I wanted to tell him that wasn't true. I wanted to say he couldn't blame stuff like that on other people, because my dad had been there, too, had gotten messed up and still had bad dreams but that he was doing his job, taking care of us . . .

But I didn't, because somehow I knew it wouldn't help and would only make things worse. I also knew it wasn't exactly true because the same things hadn't happened to my dad. He hadn't done the things Jake's dad did, and what the hell did I know, anyway? So all I said was, "He caught you, didn't he? When you were gonna try and mess up his garden."

His head jerked up and down. "I-I came through the woods, at night. But he was there, in the garden . . . in the goddamn pond, prayin' or chantin' or some goddamn thing . . . "

My stomach grew very cold and tight, thinking about what I'd seen, Mr. Trung praying in the koi pond and the koi praying to him . . .

" . . . I tried to sneak back out again but it was like he had goddamn eyes inna back of his head and he could move like the fuckin wind because suddenly he was there. He was there and he grabbed my collar and spun me around, threatenin' to call the cops . . . "

He sucked in a deep breath, composing himself. When he looked up at me, his face looked so miserable and alone my stomach twisted even tighter. "God, I wished he'd just called the cops, anythin' but . . . "

Mr. Trung.

Praying in the koi pond.

The koi praying to him.

I licked my lips and my voice came out thin and rasping. "What did he do?"

"That game," he croaked, "he made me play that goddamn game from the yard sale. That goddamn gook bastard knew I was gonna be there and he wanted me to see it, so I'd wanna play it again . . . "

Another chill passed through me. I remembered the way Mr. Trung had stared at Jake, barely looking at Kevin or me. I remembered the way he'd caressed the lid of that black wooden box and remembered the way those white ivory tiles had gleamed in sun. "What happened?"

He shrugged. "He said he'd let me go and wouldn't call the cops if I played one game with him, a simple little game with just a simple little bet . . . "

"Your dad's soul," I finished, still not understanding but, for some reason, believing despite the impossibility of it all. "You drew the tile with the bird on it . . . what was it called? Phung."

Another jerky nod. "I thought he was fuckin' bullshittin' about the game, right? That he was fuckin' crazy and the game looked so fuckin' easy so I thought 'What the hell? Why not?' But it wasn't easy, he dealt them tiles too fast and talked too fast, and I didn't understand halfa what he said. It was like the symbols on them tiles were movin' and *changin'* and before you know it I . . . I drew that damned eagle tile or whatever, but Mr. Trung said he wouldn't take *my* soul but someone else's, so I'd always know it was my fault . . . "

"Your dad," I again whispered. "But how, Jake? How could he take your dad's soul, and howdya . . . howdya know . . . ?"

He shot me a cutting gaze so filled with rage that I sidled back, feeling threatened in a way I never had before. "You don't *know*," he growled, eyes narrowing into dark slits, face twisting into an angry sneer. "You don't know what my dad's *done* since then, to us . . . and *God*, to Emma. He's never done that sorta stuff before and now he's . . . he's . . . doin *things*, the kinda things make you wanna . . . "

I held myself very still; mouth clamped shut, stomach roiling. The implications set my teeth on edge and made me feel like vomiting.

Jake had started rocking back and forth, his teeth chattering, as if he were gripped by a bone-deep cold. "He's never done them things before, *ever*. But that's all he's done since that night. He lost his job at the mill and he don't never sleep no more . . . . just drinks and bounces round the house and goes out back and pretends he's huntin' VC, snappin' shots from his rifle at anythin' that moves . . . "

Jake stopped rocking and sat up very straight, his face hardening like stone. "And it's all that gook's fault. He tricked me and took my dad's soul. His gook cousins messed my dad up in Vietnam and he took my dad's soul away and made him into some sorta . . . . *monster*."

Maybe it was the eeriness of the night, hiding behind Mr. Trung's blueberry bushes, or maybe it was the dread ringing in Jake's voice, that and the memory of Mr. Trung praying in the koi pond . . .

And the koi praying to him.

. . . or the way Mr. Trung stared at Jake the other day with his dark eyes, as if Kevin and I weren't even there. Maybe it was a combination of all these things on an especially deep and dark Adirondack night . . .

But I believed every word. "What are you gonna do?"

Jake sniffed and wiped his nose with the back of his hand, suddenly seeming nothing more than the fourteen year old he was. He nodded toward the far side of Mr. Trung's trailer, where the flower gardens and koi ponds were. "He keeps that little box in a stone chest out inna garden, under that little hut-thingy or whatever."

"Gazebo," I whispered. "It's called a gazebo."

"Whatever-the-fuck. Anyway, I been watchin' from here almost every night since then and he's always gone real late on Wednesday nights. I'm goin' in there and I'm bustin' inta that stone chest . . . "

He reached behind him, unzipped his backpack and pulled out a short-handled, hand-held sledgehammer. He hefted it, like he was Thor and it was Mjölnir. "I'm bustin' in there and gettin' that box and I'm crushin' all those tiles to fuckin' powder. I dunno how I know it, but I do. Dad's soul is trapped in them things, and I'm gonna let it out."

He looked at me then, his eyes big and wide and pleading. "Couldja look out for me?" He laid the mini-sledge on the ground, reached back into his backpack and withdrew two flashlights. He held one out to me. "You don' hafta come with me. I wouldn't ask you to do that. Just crawl down to the end of this row. If someone comes, whistle and flash twice or somethin'. That's all I'm askin'. Promise me, Nate, that you won't bail and leave me if someone comes."

We've all experienced moments of overload in our lives. Times when circumstances overwhelm us and pile one impossible factor upon another until we're so totally overwhelmed that independent thought becomes impossible. It was so that night. I'd been pushed over the line. There was no question that I'd take the flashlight and stand watch for Jake. It was the only thing he'd ever asked of me.

I stared at him for several wordless seconds, the night heavy and silent around us. Then I took the flashlight and Jake slid past me and into the night, and I never saw him up close ever again.

FIFTEEN

I CROUCHED AT the edge of those blueberry bushes, quietly afraid. Jake left his bike with me, hoisted his backpack over his shoulder, hefted his hammer once more and melted into the darkness soundlessly like a cat.

I couldn't help but shiver, thinking about Dad saying James Burns could do the same thing as a kid. That's why he'd been picked to be a Green Beret, because he could fade into the misty Cambodian jungles like he'd never been there at all. Here Jake was, doing the same, leaving me alone. The night closed in around me, darker than I'd ever seen it, so dark I could barely make out my hand.

After what seemed like forever finally it came: the sharp ring of metal striking stone, Jake swinging away at that stone chest under the gazebo. On the first strike every muscle in my body tensed. I gripped the flashlight so hard my knuckles ached, expecting the shrill sound and its echoes to bring *something* from either the shadowed depths of the blueberry bushes or from Mr. Trung's trailer. However, several more strikes rang through the night and nothing happened, so I relaxed. Mr. Trung's house was far enough away from anything on Bassler Road in either direction, so there was little chance of anyone hearing the sounds. Comforted a little in this, I hunkered down in the blueberry bushes and waited.

One more singing strike.

And then silence, filled with nothing but chirping peepers, and then . . .

Frogs.

Bullfrogs. Only one or two at first, but their throaty calls quickly multiplied into a belching chorus that, unbelievably enough, raised pimples along my forearms.

Because they came from the flower garden.

The koi pond. A pond only about ten feet in diameter. I had no idea how deep the pond was (the crazy, insane idea that it was bottomless flitted through my head,) but it didn't seem nearly big enough to hold all those frogs . . .

Then Jake screamed.

High and shrill, and it wasn't the scream of someone scared during a movie, or someone riding the water tubes over at Water Safari in Old Forge, or even the scream of someone afraid for their life. It was the scream of someone losing their mind. Somewhere in a primitive corner of my being, I knew that scream came from a mind that had shattered into a senseless ruin.

I'm not proud of what I did next.

Because it made me the man I am today.

I grabbed my bike, clumsily mounted it, plunged out of the blueberry bushes and wobbled down the night-shrouded hill leading toward Bassler Road. For several panic-stricken moments I thought for sure I'd lose control and smash into something I couldn't see or ride straight into the ditch. Somehow, I held my course true. As I flashed past Mr. Trung's carport I turned the handles just enough to veer onto the smooth blacktop driveway. Throwing caution away I practically stood up on the pedals, pumping for all I was worth.

I'm still not exactly sure what I saw, speeding past Mr. Trung's trailer and the flower gardens. I remember pale green light, almost like fog, curling up from the koi pond into the night. I remember the unnatural grumbling, belching bullfrogs, their throaty burps pounding against my brain like a jackhammer.

And I thought I saw—from the corner of my eye— Jake stumbling away from something emerging from the koi pond. I don't remember much besides glimpses of glistening hide in that pale, green glow . . . something *walking* upright, like a man . . .

Something like a bullfrog walking on two feet, like a man.

But it wasn't a man.

And I don't know how I could have possibly seen that in such a fleeting glance, but I know . . . in my heart, I *know* . . .

It wasn't a man.

My bike thumped off Mr. Trung's driveway and onto Bassler Road. I turned toward home and pedaled furiously. My heart pounded with a white-hot mindless fear as Jake screamed again.

And I sped away.

SIXTEEN

SOMEHOW I MADE it in the house undetected. Dad had gone to bed, sleeping soundly as always. Amy hadn't come home yet from hanging out with her friends. Mind and body numb, arms and legs limp, I managed to stow my bike against the garage, sneak inside without waking Dad up, and somehow crawl into bed without a sound.

Believe it or not, I fell asleep almost instantly. I'd expended all my energy in my mad dash home. Overloaded, my mind also shut down. I burrowed deep into the covers, closed my eyes and dropped into the black abyss of sleep.

But it was not restful.

I dreamed. Worse yet, I couldn't wake myself up. Instead of dreaming and jolting awake, my mind slogged through a nightmare that I couldn't drag myself free of. A nightmare of being Jake and swinging at that stone chest under the gazebo in Mr. Trung's flower garden . . .

I swing and swing, repeatedly hitting the lid to the stone chest under Mr. Trung's pagoda, hating that goddamn gook bastard with every breath and heartbeat but also ashamed because I know it's my fault because I lied to Nate and told him Mr. Trung tricked me but he gave me a *choice* and I was chicken-shit and said 'Dad' and it's all my fault that he lost his job and that he's drinking all time and hurting me and doing those things to Emma, all my fault . . .

Swing.

Rock sings against metal.

All my *fault.*

Swing.

All my *fault.*

One last swing and unbelievably enough the chest's stone lid shatters like it's made of flint or slate or something and I drop my hand-sledge, knock aside shards of stone, reach in and grab that box . . .

And I almost drop it, because it feels . . . alive. Not wood but something soft and wet, squirming in my grip, like I'm holding onto something thick and leathery, something that lives and hides in deep, dark and wet places, but fuck that. I'm the guy that finds hiding things and drags them out, just like my dad did, so I bite my tongue and pull that thing out . . .

And there's that damned wooden box.

Hands shaking I set the box on the ground in front of me, flip the lid's silver catch and slowly open it to reveal those gleaming white tiles, blank just like they were the first time that fucking goddamn gook made me play. I remember how the designs appeared after I started playing and the fear that I'd pick the wrong one that would end the game before it started . . .

I squeeze my hand to stop the shaking, then reach into the box. Just like last time the tiles feel slimy, not like ivory at all and as I pull the first tile from the box a design shimmers on it, almost like some invisible hand is writing it as I pull it out, and the design is . . .

No!

I drop the tile and I realize the light on the box and the tiles isn't from my flashlight it's weird and green and there's something squishing around behind me. I turn and scream, seeing nothing but a puckering mouth surrounded by waving, coiling things reaching for my face . . .

I sat up with sharp cry, throwing my hands out to ward off what I'd dreamed were dozens of snake-like things slithering through the air toward me . . .

I saw nothing but my room, dim and hazy with the dawn's light creeping through my window. I flopped onto my back and stared at the ceiling, desperately trying to convince myself that it had been a bad dream, nothing but a bad dream . . . but in my heart, I knew it had been *real*. Somehow I'd not seen but rather *lived* through Jake Burn's last moments here in this world.

SEVENTEEN

FOR SEVERAL DAYS afterward I stumbled about half-aware of the world around me, hard at work convincing myself that I certainly hadn't seen what I'd thought I had. I *couldn't* have. There hadn't been legions of bullfrogs croaking in Mr. Trung's koi pond, it had only sounded that way. That hadn't been a strange pale green mist floating up from the pond and filling the flower gardens. It had been a motion lamp from the back of Mr. Trung's trailer, tripped by Jake skulking around in the flower gardens, and the lamp had lit up the fog and mists.

Most importantly, there *hadn't* been something squishing its way out of the koi pond. Jake hadn't been screaming. I *hadn't* glimpsed something wet and glistening in the light. *Obviously* Mr. Trung had moved his car and hid, waiting for Jake to make his move, and had jumped out and surprised him. That's why Jake screamed.

Obviously.

Regardless, I spent Thursday and Friday drifting from one activity to another. As luck would have it, Dad had lots of chores for me those two days. I spent them mostly mowing and raking the lawn, splitting and stacking firewood, re-painting the garage and the tool sheds. Late Friday afternoon, Dad took off work and I helped him re-shingle parts of our roof.

If Dad noticed my withdrawal from the world and especially my friends those two days, he didn't mention it. I'm somewhat quiet and withdrawn to begin with, so I'm sure my dazed aloofness didn't seem so odd. But I passed on fishing with the guys Thursday afternoon, claiming chores and working in the garden. I didn't want to go fishing and see Jake *not* show up (irony of ironies).

Friday morning I passed up an invitation to bale hay with Bobby because I had to split and stack wood in the morning. *That's* why I declined, *not* because I was afraid of Jake *not showing up*.

The nights were full of dark dreams about wet things living deep in watery pools. I didn't sleep well, so I found myself dozing under the trees on the edge of our property in between chores. Unfortunately, those naps weren't all that restful either, because every time I closed my eyes I was Jake again, swinging away at that stone chest. I'd have to jerk myself awake to avoid the rest of the nightmare.

Saturday morning came. Almost against my will, I found myself bouncing out of bed, hurrying through breakfast, hopping on my bike and heading down to the Commons Yard Sale. Though a part of me didn't want to go, some strange, undeniable urge *pulled* me there. Maybe, on some instinctual level, I realized I couldn't hide indefinitely. I had to rejoin society sometime, even though the risk was learning that Jake Burns had disappeared, never to be seen or heard of again.

SOPHAN

Somehow I wasn't surprised to find myself once more standing before Mr. Trung's table. Today, however, he displayed mostly pints of freshly picked blueberries, as well as neatly ordered stacks of paperback novels. Immensely relieved to see no black wooden box (but maybe also strangely disappointed) I moved past Mr. Trung's table, ready to leave it behind . . .

When I encountered it against the table's far end.

A bike.

Leaning against the end of Mr. Trung's table, with a price tag hanging from its handlebars. It looked brand new and recently painted a metallic blue, but I recognized the diamond-fractal reflection plate protruding from the steering column.

Jake's bike.

A thought occurred to me then. A cold, dreadful type of awareness that changed the way I thought about the world forever. Mr. Trung had sold *other* seemingly brand new bikes here, every summer. And worse . . .

He'd sell more.

I stared at that terribly familiar metallic-blue bike that became even more familiar with each passing minute. I might've stared indefinitely if I'd not heard the soft, rustling voice of Mr. Trung.

"Master Nate? Are you all right?"

I spun and gaped. There stood Mr. Trung, behind his yard sale table, gently holding that black wooden box inscribed with silver-inlaid symbols. Even today, I can't properly describe the expression I saw on his soft, lightly wrinkled round face. He smiled gently, cheeks dimpling and he looked kind and forgiving . . .

But something *hungry* glittered in those eyes. It was then I knew, without a shadow of a doubt, that everything I'd seen Wednesday night had been real. Worse yet . . . Mr. Trung *knew* I'd been there, somehow, and knew I'd seen.

"Is there anything I can get you, Master Nate? A few pints of blueberries, perhaps?"

I managed to shake my head on its fear-frozen neck. "No thanks," I rasped.

"Well then," he whispered, smile widening into something unpleasant, "perhaps you'd like to pass the time playing a round of Sốphận."

He extended the box toward me. And to this day, I swear on my life the silver-inlaid design on its lid was *moving*.

Like it was alive.

I don't remember much after that. I spun away and blundered through the yard sale crowd, somehow making it to my bike at the Commons entrance. I frantically pedaled home. I'm not ashamed to admit that for a good part of the way I sobbed in fear, my heart threatening to burst from my chest. When home I flung my bike onto its side in the driveway, scrambled away and made for the woods. I spent the next three hours tramping along the railroad tracks that ran behind our house, feeling safe only because I knew the woods surrounding the tracks was mostly dry land, and there weren't any bodies of water for miles.

EIGHTEEN

J AKE BURNS WAS never seen in Clifton Heights again. The news broke in the churches that Sunday morning, the local pastors requesting prayer for James Burns because it appeared that his only son Jake had 'run away.' Kevin called me about it later that afternoon.

Amazingly enough I felt nothing at all, initially. I'd returned from my journey along the railroad tracks Saturday exhausted, drained, my mind emptied. I passed a restful night after a quiet evening listening to old re-runs of *The Shadow* on AM radio while cooking hotdogs over the campfire with Dad and Amy.

I knew Jake hadn't run away (or at least I thought I did) but something had happened in my head on that long, mostly forgotten ramble along the railroad tracks. The terror had leaked away, leaving only vague images and impressions. I never shared with my friends what I *thought* I'd seen that night. I agreed with their assumption that Jake had finally decided to flee the domestic abuse all of us so tactfully never discussed.

The days passed. Our mundane but moderately charmed summer existence continued unabated. It became much easier to deny what I'd seen. I accepted what I wanted to, what everyone else thought: that Jake Burns had run away.

Somehow, I often wonder if that was truer than even I knew.

Certain things did change, however. I never picked blueberries at Mr. Trung's again. Throughout the rest of my childhood and into my teens, I avoided his property like the plague. Also, I decided I didn't much like fishing or swimming or any activities involving large bodies of natural water after that. Honestly, even to this day, swimming in man-made, filtered, chlorine saturated pools gives me a bad turn.

Not long after that, James Burns was re-hired at the lumber mill. According to Dad, Jake running away must've served as a catalyst for change because James Burns joined the local chapter of AA, started getting counseling and started *trying*, at least, to live a cleaner life. I can't say that he ever became a model citizen or that his daughter Emma instantly morphed into bubbling, successful social butterfly. She, in fact, turned into a first-generation brooding, black-haired, black lipstick wearing death-metal-head banging Goth. But her dad started trying, at least, which makes me wonder if somehow Jake was successful in releasing his dad's soul, or if some sort of . . . trade took place.

What happened to Mr. Trung?

Partway through the summer before my freshman year in college Pastor Ward found Mr. Trung floating face down in his koi pond. Our local newspaper reported it as a heart attack due to overexertion on a hot summer day.

I suppose that's possible, even likely. By then he

was nearly seventy. It had been almost eighty degrees that day. Everyone accepted the story at face value; it wasn't the first time an elderly person had passed away in such a fashion due to the heat. The consensus around town, of course, was that he'd at least passed away doing what he loved.

But there were rumors, too.

About how Pastor Ward had originally sworn (but later recanted) that *something* had darted away from Mr. Trung's floating body, into the pond's depths. Also, that Mr. Trung's face had been chewed up considerably, that something had gnawed on his face from underwater. The rumors faded pretty quickly, but no one ever expressed any interest in buying that land, to my knowledge.

Even though I swore I wouldn't, I looked at Mr. Trung's obituary in the newspaper. Can't say I was surprised to see that not only had he emigrated from Vietnam—where he'd lost his children and his wife to the war—but he'd also served in the Southern Vietnamese Army and had done time as a prisoner of war for the U. S.

Those Wednesday 'meetings' he'd always attended? A support group for emotionally suffering veterans. Whether or not he and Jake's dad actually crossed paths in the war, or at those meetings, I have no way of knowing. But seeing that in his obituary added a whole new layer of mystery.

An odd thing: Though local kids are always braving the ruins of Old Bassler House, no one dares set foot on Mr. Trung's old property. Could be there's just nothing left to explore, seeing as how someone long ago carted the trailer away for salvage.

However, I think . . . I *know*, in the pit of my gut . . . it's more than that. There's *something* in the air here that keeps children away. I can *feel* that something now. But I didn't come here to shy away from Sõphân, my fate. I came here to meet it head on, confront it finally and either rid my life of this stain forever . . .

Or pay the price for my sins.

Before the pond stands Jake, looking exactly as he did the last night I saw him. He's really upset now, again waving toward Bassler Road, begging me to leave, glancing down every few seconds at the koi pond, as if expecting something to rise from its depths at any moment.

I first saw Jake at the beginning of this summer. On the first official day, actually, I caught a brief glimpse of him standing in the driveway when Dad and I got home from work one night. Just a flash, there one moment, gone the next. I brushed the whole thing off as a tired mind dredging up random images.

I awoke that night to see phantom Jake standing over my bed, staring down at me. And the strange thing was, I felt no fear. I looked at him, offered him a small smile and whispered, "So this is how it's gonna be, huh?" The ghost-Jake nodded slowly, face unreadable. I rolled over and fell back asleep.

I've seen him almost every day since then, in odd places. Standing alongside the road near creeks we used to fish in. At the lumber mill a lot, which makes sense, I suppose, seeing as how his dad used to work there. I started back haying this summer, now with

Bobby Drake instead of his dad, and I often see Jake then, too, trailing after the wagon, or lounging on a bale of hay in the barn as we stack.

At first I thought my mind was starting to throw a few gears. But when my package came the other day and Jake showed up, waving his arms frantically, looking desperate to keep me away from the mail, I finally accepted Jake—whatever he is: ghost, phantom, echo—as being real.

And right now, standing there by the old koi pond, waving desperately, shooting wary glances at the pond's scummy waters, he looks more terrified than I've ever seen him. His expression shoots cold ripples up the back of my neck, but I'm ignoring them. This *must* be done. I can't go on like this, anymore. Nothing has been the same since that night. I pretended to brush off Jake's disappearance like everyone else. I buried memories of that night and that bright green mist and Jake's screams and that wet, glistening thing.

But on the inside things were all *wrong*. I went through the motions and studied hard and watched monster movies with Bill Ward and kept doing all the things everyone wanted me to do: my teachers, my guidance counselors, my friends, and especially my dad. I danced the dance and sang the song, enough to make everyone happy and to convince myself, on the *surface* anyway, that things were fine.

But I hollowed out a little more every year, became a little emptier inside as time passed. No nightmares or anything like that. I wouldn't have called myself *afraid*, actually. More like intensely apathetic. Life had lost its flavor. I drifted along, feeling very distant from everything, out of touch, wondering when someone would notice.

Through the rest of high school, no one did. I eased scot-free through college, graduating with a Bachelor's Degree in Science, which basically meant I wasn't qualified for any career, really. I'd earned lukewarm grades, having drifted through my studies as I'd drifted through life. After graduation I returned home to live with Dad and work at the one place I'd always feared I'd end up: the lumber mill.

Things have been fine for the past ten years or so, mostly. Quiet. Uneventful. I think occasionally Dad wonders what happened. I know he'd always hoped I'd end up somewhere else, doing something better. However, I also think he's just thankful for the company, with Amy married and moved away. We actually get along better now than we ever have, which makes a strange kind of sense. I'm scarred now, too. Though he's never asked how or why I think he recognizes that, somehow, and it's brought us closer.

But as I've said, yesterday I received a package in the mail with no return postage. If anyone's reading this, I imagine you've already guessed what the package contained: that wooden black box containing those gleaming white tiles with the strange designs that seem to shift in the light. At least I assume they're in there, based on the box's heft and the sound of them clinking together inside. I haven't exactly opened it yet.

Because I'm afraid. Nothing has really been right with my life since I left Jake behind to face . . . whatever rose from the koi pond. Who knows? Maybe I could've done something to help Jake. Maybe he'd be alive today if I'd tried. Or maybe I would've disappeared right along with him.

The point is, I did nothing. I *ran*. I *left* Jake and, because of that, I've been living an empty life ever since. And here, mysteriously, sent to me by some unknown party is that same black box Jake had been searching for that night, the one containing that tile game of Mr. Trung's. Sõphạn, the game Jake claimed had stolen his father's soul, the game he was hoping to destroy to release it.

I failed Jake that night. I could've helped him. Could've done *something*, at least. Instead I ran. So it's time to belly up to the bar for one last drink. Time to face the proverbial music, because I lost something that night, too. I'm not sure how, but when Jake disappeared I think a little bit of *my* soul got sucked away with him, either because of something mystical, or because I'd traded a piece of it away in my selfish escape.

I don't know how the box made it back to me. Regardless, after all these years it's finally time to play the game. And if I win, if I wipe the slate clean, no one will ever have to read this.

If I lose?

Somebody please burn this goddamn garden and gazebo down, drain the pond, fill it with concrete. And if you find the box, for God's sake *don't* open it. Just burn it. *Please*.

I imagine this is how it'll go: I'll put my flashlight down, aiming the light to illuminate a patch of the pagoda's concrete steps. I'll set down the black box and open it, then remove the tiles and arrange them on the concrete before me, in hopes of putting Jake's soul to rest after all this time.

Next I'll stack the tiles, and as those etched designs glow and pulse I'll try my best to ignore the rippling and squishing sounds that are sure to come from wet footsteps ascending the koi pond's steps.

Regardless of the outcome, I know this: I feel a sort of peace, because soon, it'll be over.

Finally.

THE SKYLARK DINER

FATHER WARD CLOSES the journal but doesn't look up for several minutes as he taps its cover with a fingertip. His expression looks similar to the one I've always imagined wearing after finishing Gavin's latest batch of stories: one of incredulous, amazed unease.

Of course, neither Father Ward nor Fitzy has read many of Gavin's stories. They apparently decided early on there was a limit to what they wanted to "know" about this town. It's become understood that Gavin's stories are strictly for him and I. This story, however, *felt* intended for Father Ward. At the very least, he figured so largely in it I believed he needed to read it.

When Father Ward still hadn't spoken after another minute, I broke the silence. "When's the last time you saw Nate Slocum?"

Father Ward glances at me, his expression thoughtful. "Months. Think maybe I ran into him at The Great American one day, buying groceries. We chatted briefly about nothing in particular. He seemed okay. I mean, not bouncing and full of life . . . but okay."

His brow wrinkles. "Have you called his father?"

"I have. The morning after we found this, Nate turned up missing. He left no note, nothing's been packed, all his stuff is still in his room. His dad's worried, understandably. Has been concerned about Nate for a while, apparently. Seems he's been quieter than usual, ever since . . . "

" . . . the beginning of summer," Father Ward finishes quietly, "when he started seeing Jake Burns."

"What about Jake? Remember much about him?"

Father Ward shakes his head. "Not really. Just the minor furor when he ran away. The only kids in that grade I knew were Nate and Kevin Ellison."

"Should I run this by Kevin? Ask him a few questions? Seems like he was pretty close to Nate back then."

Father Ward shakes his head decisively. "I wouldn't. Kevin's father just passed away. I imagine he's pretty busy settling affairs. School doesn't start for a few more weeks and he's still taking a leave of absence for most of September."

Gears click in my head. "Right. Brian Ellison. I knew that. Just didn't make the connection between the two."

Cassie Tillman (who always seems to be waitressing no matter when we visit) had long since taken our orders (the blueberry pancake special for us both) and she chooses this moment to deliver them. She offers us both a familiar smile but doesn't say much as she sets down our plates. Then she's off like a quiet gust of wind to another booth across the diner.

We eat mostly in silence. When Father Ward is halfway finished, he sets his fork down and wipes his mouth thoughtfully with a napkin. He raises his cup of coffee, sips and says, looking at something far away, "I remember the day my father found Mr. Trung in his koi pond. I'd never seen him so . . . disturbed, before. He came home from the police station, went straight into the bedroom with Mother, locked the door and spent the next hour or so quietly arguing with her about . . . something. Back then, I had no idea what, but now I imagine it was whatever he thought he saw in that koi pond when he found Mr. Trung. Probably called the police station and changed his story right after talking with Mother."

He takes another sip. "Honestly, I don't remember folks spreading rumors about something in the koi pond at all. All I remember is folks saying how sad it was that Mr. Trung passed away alone, and that's it."

He sets his cup down and looks at me with slightly narrowed eyes. "The journal and the flashlight were the only things found at the scene? Not the . . . game. Sỗphận, was it called?"

I sip my coffee, swallow and say, "No game. No tiles. Just the flashlight next to the journal. That's all."

Father Ward nods and says, "If we take this story at face value . . . I don't believe Mr. Trung was . . . evil."

I shake my head wearily. This town's *grayness* is something I'm still getting used to. "According to Slocum's account—*if* we take it at face value—Mr. Trung did *something* to Jake Burns. Maybe did things to other kids, too. I checked the records. Several other boys Jake's age disappeared in the years previous to Jake."

Father Ward purses his lips and gives me a look. "That's not so surprising, given this town. You know that."

I nod, smiling grimly. "True. But I dug deeper. Those other boys that went missing? A bunch of them had fathers who'd served in Vietnam, also."

Father Ward sighs, reaching for his fork. "There's a fine line between hurting others because you've been hurt, and then hurting others because . . . you've come to *like* it. I suppose we'll never know if Mr. Trung crossed that line."

With that he falls silent and works on his pancakes. I follow suit, finding that, surprisingly enough, the pancakes taste just fine despite our macabre conversation. What that says about our ability to adapt, I don't like to think about too much.

After Cassie Tillman returns with our check and takes our plates, however, I can't help but mutter, "This town, huh? It never ends, does it?"

Father Ward sits back, rests his hands on his stomach, opens his mouth to speak . . . but stops. That same preoccupied expression from when he first entered The Skylark returns. It's then I realize something: Father Ward has something of his own to share, for a change.

"What is it?"

Father Ward shakes his head, hesitates, and then says slowly, "Maybe . . . maybe it's not JUST this town."

I sit up straighter. "What do you mean?"

Father Ward tips his head and looks out the window, over The Skylark's front parking lot. "Clifton Heights has its . . . secrets. Things happen here. Strange things, and we seem to . . . *know* more about these things than the average citizen. But that doesn't mean we're the only town with secrets, the only place where odd and unexplainable things happen. These things must happen elsewhere. It only makes sense."

He turns and looks at me. I can see it, in his eyes: Father Ward has moved from passive observer and spiritual supporter to an active receiver of the strange, like Gavin and me. "Ever heard of Tahawus? Small little town to the north? Know a man named Stuart Michael Evans?"

I shake my head. "Nothing on both counts."

"What about The Can Man? The can and bottle recycling place out on Route 434? Ever been there?"

"Sure. Most everyone has."

"Ever see the guy working there with the limp? Medium height, skinny, longish hair, narrow face with deep-set eyes? And I mean *serious* limp. Both feet are pointed inward."

I sit back and think for a moment. Sure enough, a vague mental image forms. "Think so. He wears a lot of those classic eighties and nineties rock'n roll T-shirts, right? Metallica, Judas Priest, Motley Crue, L. A. Guns?"

Father Ward nods. "That's him. He came to All Saints last night. At least, I'm nearly certain it was him, based on the story he told me. As for that . . . "

I nod slowly, clarity dawning, crystal clear. "One of *those* kinds of stories, right?"

"Yes, *absolutely*. Now, understand. He's not Catholic, so he didn't ask to confess his sins under the Sacrament of Penance. That's the *only* reason I'm able to tell you this, right? In fact . . . I'm not sure, but I believe he *wanted* me to tell someone about this. He felt the world had to know, and he asked me to do . . . to do something after he'd told me his story."

I nod. "Sure. Go on."

"It was near time for me to close the church. In fact, I was just about to leave the confessional when I heard this rhythmic clicking come down the aisle, as if someone handicapped was using a walker. I waited for a moment. Sure enough that clicking sound stopped at the confessional. Someone stepped inside, settled themselves and said . . . "

THE MAN IN
YELLOW

ONE

... SO I'M NOT sure how this goes. 'Forgive me Father, for I have sinned?' Except I'm not Catholic. I'm not much of anything, anymore."

I leaned closer to the confessional grate, amused. Back when I was fresh out of seminary I might've offered a mild rebuke or advised the penitent to seek counsel at either the institution of their denomination, or from a professional counselor. However, after years of experience I've come to realize that sometimes folks simply need relief from their burdens. These days I'm more than happy to offer an ear, regardless of their denomination, or lack thereof.

"That's quite all right. You've come here because you need comfort. I can't promise you freedom from pain in this life, or that I've any advice that'll solve your problems. I can promise, however, that I'll listen and offer you what comfort I can."

The man shifted on the cushions in the adjoining booth. "Thanks, Father. This isn't a problem anyone can solve, really. It's just ... " More shifting, and then, "like you said: release. I gotta tell somebody. Been living with it for over twenty years, and I gotta tell somebody now, before—"

"Before what? Tell me, if you can."

The man's shadowed profile hung its head on the other side of the grate. "Father? Have you ever done something terrible that was also something that *had* to be done, to prevent something even worse?"

I nodded slowly, even though the gesture couldn't be seen. "I served as an Army Chaplain in Afghanistan for four years. I saw soldiers struggle with things they'd done, and, like you, grapple with the reality that if they *hadn't* acted, even worse consequences might have ensued."

The shadowed profile nodded. "Exactly. I didn't want to do it. Hell no, I didn't. But if I hadn't, if I'd just let it spread . . . "

For some reason, the man's frantic tone made me uneasy. I felt compelled to warn, "Think very carefully about what you want to share. Are you asking for the Sacrament of Penance? If so, what you share will remain confidential. I'm bound by my office and faith never to divulge a word. If not, however . . . ."

"No, Father . . . someone needs to know about this. *People* need to know about this, so I don't care if you tell anyone else after. I just want to sit here and tell *you* first."

"Tell me what?"

"Tell you how it all started, the first night of Vacation Bible School, after my senior year in high school . . .

" . . . how it all started with *faith*."

TWO

I GREW UP in Tahawus, a small town here in the Adirondacks. If you've never heard of it, Father, don't feel bad. Tahawus didn't have much in the way of . . . well, anything. At a population of barely a hundred, we weren't exactly a planned stop on anyone's tourist agenda.

Which was okay, I suppose. Old Forge and Lake George are nice enough, but in the summers especially, their sidewalks are always swamped with city folks who'd decided on a "wilderness" vacation only to spend it browsing kitschy knick-knack stores jammed full of cheap novelty items. In Tahawus, we had none of that, so far off the beaten path. Hardly anyone from outside ever came to town, save occasional product deliveries to our small stores. Mostly, folks either graduated from Tahawus High, stayed there to raise families, or they left for college and never returned.

We didn't even have a police force of our own. The nearest state police barracks was over an hour away in Woodgate. We only saw them on their random, semi-monthly drive-bys. Honestly, there was no *reason* to see them. Nothing very important ever happened in Tahawus, really.

Not before the man in yellow came to town, anyway.

In any case, isolated was the word. To the north of us, the closest town—Big Moose Lake—was an hour and a half away. To the east and west stood nothing but dense Adirondack forest cut by narrow, winding backcountry roads that led who knew where. To the south, Clifton Heights was only forty minutes away, the nearest town.

But the isolation wasn't so bad, really. No tourists crowding the sidewalks in the summer. No college kids from Adirondack Community or Utica Tech or Plattsburg or Web Community hitting our two bars to blow off steam on the weekends. It was only us. We liked that just fine.

And for such a small town, folks pretty much minded their own business. Everyone knew each other but they didn't necessarily know *everything* everyone did, save the normal gossips all small towns have. Mostly, folks in Tahawus knew *circumstances*. Usually, that was a good thing. When folks fell on hard times, people in our town helped. All one hundred of them, nearly. When Mom passed, back when I was nine, the ladies of Tahawus kept us in covered dish meals and home-baked cookies and pies for months.

We were a tight-knit community. Quite honestly, faith had a lot to do with that. We weren't a holy-rolling, Bible-thumping town by any means, but a common faith bound us together. As son of the town's only pastor, I saw that from a front row seat. The people of Tahawus had faith in each other and some Higher Power. Some held beliefs more nuanced than others, but even so. Nearly everyone in town attended church, and those who didn't were tolerated in the spirit of "Godly love." Our monthly fellowship dinners always packed the house. So did our annual screenings of *Ben-hur* and *The Ten Commandments*. Our annual winter missionary conference and summer Vacation Bible School were the biggest events of the year. Indeed, our strong sense of faith made Tahawus what it was.

It also proved to be our undoing.

See, the funny thing about humans and faith is this: Though most definitions portray faith as something that can't be proved in any tangible way, its greatest advocates are endlessly *trying* to prove it. Despite all the heartfelt assurances found in hymns and sermons, humans are always clamoring for proof of *faith* . . . aren't we?

Father, I'm sure you've noticed that my references to Tahawus are in the past tense. There's another really good reason for having never heard of us: We don't exist, anymore. Haven't since the summer of 1992. All that remains of Tahawus are abandoned and boarded up homes, stores, the school and the crumbling ashes of my father's church. What was it that killed Tahawus, in the end?

Faith.

Or at the very least, our consuming need for it. Humans are a contradictory species. We cling onto something as intangible as faith, drawing strength from it to change history and lives on small and epic scales. However, all of us, deep down inside, really crave proof that our faith is *real*, whether we admit it or not. We can sing hymns all night long about a "faith that endureth forever" and even mean it on most levels, but in the end, no matter how righteous or kind-hearted or faithful, we all crave *proof* that our faith is in something *real*.

I could easily blame the man in yellow for our destruction. He certainly played his part. His deception, his maddening lies and malice, the way he ravaged our minds and souls . . . he certainly deserves the lion's share of the blame. He did many unspeakable things, things I'm probably unaware of to this day. I desperately wish he'd never come to our town.

But the truth of the matter is this: The seeds of our destruction had lain dormant for quite some time, waiting for the right conditions to blossom. The man in yellow—invited by us—merely provided the right conditions, sealing our fate.

It would also be easier if I could say Tahawus *had* been full of Holy Rolling Bible-Thumping Freaks so enamored with godliness that they couldn't see past the planks in their own eyes. That just wasn't the case. Tahawus was full of good people who cared. People who'd possessed a simple, generous, ardent faith.

But of course, Tahawus had also been full of *humans*. Compassionate, generous, giving and self-sacrificing . . . but *weak*. When the man in yellow offered us the secret things we all desired most, we *caved*. In a matter of days Tahawus was no more. Of course, that last part was my fault.

But I had to do it.

I couldn't let it spread.

And the thing is, we weren't offered these nasty little temptations, like you might find in a Stephen King or Ted Dekker novel. Folks didn't bed their neighbor's spouses, receive mysterious envelopes full of cash, earn straight A's in exchange for their souls or get revenge on someone who'd hurt them.

No, I believe the man in yellow offered folks much subtler prizes: health. Freedom from physical and emotional pain. Acceptance. Belonging. Stronger eyesight, confident speech. Clean, clear breath. And the townspeople lapped those things up like newborn kittens drinking milk, never once considering the cost.

Because we're a strange breed, we humans. We may have faith the size of a mustard seed that can move mountains, but deep inside, we really all want to see, feel, taste and touch. When offered the chance to do so, nine times out of ten, we swallow the bait and get gutted by the hook hidden inside it.

The sad thing is, I alone survived, but only because of how weak my faith in *anything* had gotten. I survived because I was a sorry-assed cynical son of a bitch that questioned everything and trusted nothing. I survived because I'd stopped believing in anything good the day my mother died. *That's* why I survived the man in yellow's visit to Tahawus. I take very little pleasure in it, because I'm not sure exactly what it is I survived to.

But, like faith, it is what it is.

And it all started the Sunday night Bobby Simmons and I found the dead dogs.

THREE

W HAT'S THAT SMELL? *Geez.* That's nasty."
Bobby Simmons stopped on the well-worn path in
the woods behind Tahawus First Methodist, tripped
his inhaler and sucked in a wheezing breath. I stopped
and sniffed, grimacing at something that smelled sour,
like a bag of week-old fried chicken I'd once found in
our fridge. That, however, didn't begin to match this
stench, especially on a warm July evening. Whatever
we smelled had been rotting all day in 70-degree
weather. It was just off the path to our right, in the
brush somewhere.

Bobby took another wheezing hit from his inhaler,
then a swig of his Dr. Pepper. He swallowed and
squinted through fish-bowl glasses into the woods.
"Wanna check it out?"

I shrugged, following his gaze into the
undergrowth. We were skipping Sunday evening
church, like always. We'd slipped from the balcony
during opening prayers, then cut through the woods
behind First Methodist along a path to the gas station
on Wolton Road. There we bought soda and snacks.
We never made trouble, just meandered back along
the path, sipping sodas and munching Slim Jims,

musing about life. Who got caught making out at the park, Bridgette Neilson's boobs, who was the better singer—Vince Neil or Steve Tyler—the girls we liked, and if the assistant pastor's daughter was as easy as rumored.

Slipped in between celebrity boobs and the assistant pastor's daughter, we batted about semi-serious questions about God and Heaven and Hell. We wondered whether or not the Bible was true, part-true, or made-up. Though I never spoke it aloud, I treasured those walks with Bobby, because we covered just as much metaphysical ground in our own teenage way as any of Dad's sermons.

Anyway, much as I enjoyed our usual Sunday night walks, I felt mildly uneasy skipping church that night. It wasn't just Sunday evening church; it was the opening ceremonies for Vacation Bible School. Standing there in the woods, playing hookey on the first night of VBS and smelling something dead rotten? It felt like a mild rebuke from God, though I'd long ago stopped attending VBS myself.

And honestly?

Something about that rotten smell felt *wrong*. Foul. Unclean. Things probably died and rotted behind the church all the time. That was just Nature. Even so, I felt very tempted to decline Bobby's invitation to "check it out."

But teenage boys avoid any semblance of "chickening out" like the plague. I shrugged again, sipped at my Coke and pointed at what looked like a break in the growth, feeling equal parts repelled and fascinated. "Sure. Looks like something went through here, and the smell's that way." I waved my bottle at the trampled bushes. "Lead on, Nancy Drew."

Bobby smiled in good humor and did so. In hindsight, I feel some shame about always letting him go first, though I had good reason to. The cerebral palsy that hitched my walk into a sideways gait always made me worried about my footing. When your feet perpetually point inward at a 45-degree angle, they trip really easy.

Bobby pushed his glasses higher up on his nose, sucked on his inhaler, ducked his head under a branch and moved into the undergrowth. He thoughtfully held back the branch for me as I stumbled behind him into a small clearing. An acrid wall of stench stopped me in my tracks, bringing actual tears to my eyes.

"Holy s-shit," Bobby wheezed. He jammed his inhaler into his mouth and took another blast.

I swallowed, my mouth tasting faintly of bile. "I'll second that. What the *fuck* is this?"

Dogs.

Dead dogs. Two of them. Though I had a hard time believing my eyes, they looked . . . skinned. Their tails had been chopped off. Dark red muscle gleamed wetly on flanks and haunches. Little bands of white gristle circled their joints. Blood had splattered all over the hastily cleared brush. Dozens, maybe hundreds of spots crawled over the two carcasses. No maggots yet, but with all those flies it wouldn't be long.

That, of course, was the last straw. The image of fleshy worms writhing inside those stinking bodies made my stomach churn. I was pretty sure if we didn't bail immediately, my Coke and partially devoured Slim Jim would end up all over my NIKEs. In fact, just the thought of my Slim Jim twitched my guts. I tossed the uneaten portion, still in its wrapper, away.

I grasped Bobby's elbow, weakly tugging him away. "Dude, let's split. I'm gonna chuck."

Bobby just stood there, breathing in a hypnotic, even rhythm. Despite his asthma, he just stood and stared at something in the middle of the clearing. "What . . . what's that?"

I steeled my guts and glanced back. Sure enough, something sat before the dead dogs. It looked like a statue or an altar. I didn't look at it too long—my stomach hurt and I wanted out of there—but the weird thing was, it seemed to shiver the whole time. Like it couldn't hold one shape, or my eyes couldn't make sense of the shape it was in.

I looked away, a slight headache blooming in my temples. I tugged on Bobby's arm again. "C'mon man, seriously. Let's bail. Before we puke."

By then he was looking pretty white himself. His asthma had finally kicked in, rasping in the back of his throat. I figured he was probably just as close as me to blowing chow. But, as I pulled him out of that clearing, he stared over his shoulder at that statue or shrine or whatever it was. Even after we were scurrying wordlessly down the path toward the church, I'm pretty sure I caught him repeatedly glancing over his shoulder. Like he'd missed something or lost something back there.

Like he'd wanted to stay.

FOUR

WE MADE IT back to church just as the final hymn rose into full swing. We ditched our empty soda bottles in the dumpster out back. Then we snuck around front, through the front doors, through the foyer and up the balcony stairs. Everything was going according to plan, until we peeked around the corner into the balcony and saw a man sitting in the front row who hadn't been there when we'd left.

Even sitting, he looked tall and imposing. His wide shoulders stretched his impossibly bright yellow suit jacket. Leaning just a bit farther around the corner, I caught the sunny flash of his pant leg and realized his whole suit was a blazing, almost nauseatingly bright yellow. He was leaning forward, elbows resting on his knees, chin perched on folded hands. He gazed down upon the congregation with a hungry, intense scrutiny. Like a predatory bird, I thought, stalking its unsuspecting prey.

And then, slowly . . . he smiled.

Tapping his nose with his index finger, on which glittered a ring with an enormous onyx stone. Though I couldn't see it very clearly, some sort of yellow design spiraled across that ring's gleaming black stone.

THE MAN IN YELLOW

Without speaking, Bobby and I retreated from the balcony toward the stairs to wait for the service's end there. Even though the man never once glanced in our direction, I suspected then—and I know now—that he knew we were watching, and that's why he'd been smiling.

FIVE

B OBBY AND 1 parted that night with very little to say, though at the time I'd thought that was because of the congregation's rush to the parking lot after the service. Bobby got caught up with his family, me with Dad. Looking back, however, I realize that something had already started worming its way between us, which, of course, I didn't know at the time.

I tried not to think about those dead dogs and that weird altar thing as Dad silently drove home. Like anyone faced with something they didn't understand, I wrapped it up in a little box and shoved it deep down inside me.

We were always hearing about weird stuff like that, anyway. A few years before, folks had found dead skinned cats next to the railroad tracks behind the high school. Most kids thought the abandoned barn sitting in an old cornfield on the edge of town was haunted. A ghost girl supposedly haunted Bassler Road on the way to Clifton Heights.

Every small town has its creepy stories. Even though our town was smaller than most, I figured this was just one more of those. Dead dogs found skinned in the woods behind Tahawus First Methodist Church, arranged all spooky-like before a weird altar? Probably just some punks trying to creep-out church folks. That's all.

And by the time we got home, I believed that.

Mostly.

SIX

WHEN DAD CAME to my room that night, I was doing as always before bed: strumming a few unplugged chords on my fender. The feel of strings vibrating under my fingers always helped me relax. Plus, it was my daily ritual. I was going to be a star someday, a shredder the likes of Slash or Mick Mars or Nikki Six.

Of course, I didn't have much talent. Very little separated me from thousands of other young metal heads across the country. Best I ever managed on the guitar was adequate. The biggest venue I ever played was in a Motley Crue cover band named Dr. Feelgood in the Utica bars a few years later. But still, every kid has his dream. Big-time lead guitarist of a platinum-album rock band was mine.

Anyway, that night I was strumming a classic Eagles tune—"Hotel California" —when Dad nudged my bedroom door open, leaned back against the door jamb and asked quietly, "What'd you think of Reverend Alistair's message tonight? We're awful blessed to have someone of his stature preaching for VBS this summer."

I kept my expression carefully neutral while I

picked at my fender. Even though church meant little to me, I didn't want Dad knowing about me and Bobby skipping. I also didn't want him thinking I'd paid zero attention in church the past few months—even though I hadn't—and had no clue *who* was speaking at VBS this week.

So I looked up, shrugged and said, "Okay, I guess. I dunno. We've had so many guest speakers over the years. They all kinda seem the same."

Dad frowned slightly. "Really? Even with that bright yellow suit, pulpit pounding and his accent? That's a bit unique, for us."

Oh.

Shit.

My luck this year's speaker would be some radical departure from the norm, catching me out. I nodded slowly, dancing on the razor's edge. "Well, yeah. Definitely. Maybe that was the problem. His accent made it hard to follow, I guess, and that suit . . . "

In a flash, insight hit me.

The hungry-looking man sitting in the balcony with that insanely bright yellow suit.

That must have been him. But what had he been doing in the balcony, alone? Granted, we'd snuck up there during the closing hymn, but . . .

"Yeah, that suit was something else. Like, really bright. Hey," I leaned forward—not too eagerly, though; didn't want to overplay my hand—and added, "where'd he go after his message?"

Dad's frown deepened. "Go? What do you mean?"

"Well, after he ended his message and left the podium and stage," which he must've, for us to have seen him in the balcony, "where'd he go?"

Dad folded his arms, now assuming a slightly stern air I knew too well. "He didn't go anywhere, Stuart. He stood next to me the whole time."

A bewildering sense of despair hit me. Not only did that make no sense—I'd seen *some* guy wearing a bright yellow suit sitting in the balcony—it also meant I was very likely busted.

I opened my mouth to mount some feeble defense, but Dad beat me to it, giving his officially disapproving frown. "All right, Stu. Better come clean and admit it now."

I swallowed, genuinely uneasy, not only still confused by the guy in the yellow suit but also afraid of pissing Dad off. He'd always been pretty lenient about my "faith life," despite being the pastor of First Methodist. And honestly, he'd always trusted me. Yeah, we did skip Sunday night church every week, but we never did anything bad. I didn't want to lose those outings, but I also didn't want him to be disappointed in me, either.

"And . . . admit what?"

Dad sighed, shook his head, looking every inch the regretful and disappointed preacher-dad. "No use hiding it. You've been at it for a while now. Been pretty clever about it, but I think it's time to curtail this little diversion."

I feigned confusion, though inside I *knew* I was busted. "Whaddya mean?"

He blew another exasperated sigh and gave me a pointed look. "You've been ignoring the sermons again. Writing song lyrics on the bulletin's note sections instead of paying attention . . . haven't you?"

My relief felt so ridiculously profound I had to force an abashed expression. Of course, the accusation *was* mostly true. I did usually ignore the messages in favor of toying with song lyrics on the backs of the Sunday morning bulletins. I sighed and did my best to look ashamed. "Yeah. Yeah, I have been. Sorry Dad. I've just had lots of good ideas lately and . . . "

The truthfulness of the lie made my cover story seem genuine. "These ideas have been bouncing around my head for weeks. I just needed to write them down. They always seem to hit me at church, usually because of worship." Considering our contemporary worship band—replete with electric guitars and drums—this wasn't exactly a lie, either.

Miraculously, Dad bought it. "I understand. Your mother wanted to be a writer. Did you know that?" Having heard this many times before, I nodded dutifully. "She got to be the same way before she died. Always jotting down ideas on scraps of paper, regardless of what we were doing or where we were. Sometimes, I think," and here he offered a wry grin, "even during some of my own dryer sermons."

His smile faded a bit as he glanced with mild distaste at my Dokken, Motley Crue, Tesla and Aerosmith posters. This was safe territory, however, because he was falling back on his old standby concerns. "I do wish, however, you'd think about writing a song for morning worship. You've a God-given talent with your words and that guitar. Be a shame not to use it for His glory, occasionally."

I kept my face blank, nodding. "Yeah, sure. If an idea for a worship tune comes up, I'll . . . y'know. Run it by you."

I felt sorry for Dad in a way. How he nodded his head, looking hopeful and resigned at the same time. He put his hand on the doorknob, lingering. "Stuart? Could you do me a favor this week?"

I smiled faintly, cringing inside. Mild and humble in his own way, despite being a preacher with a metal head for a son, Dad never commanded me or forced me into anything religious other than Sunday morning services. Instead, he always asked me to *do him a favor*. "Sure," I said, injecting a false note of affability into my voice, "What's up?"

"Think about attending at least one of the teen seminars this week at VBS? Maybe even bring Bobby with you. I know it's not your scene . . . but Reverend McIlvian is a special man, Mike, with special gifts. I think you'd . . . "

He paused, shifted, as always gripped by devotion and conflict. He truly and deeply believed what he preached, but he didn't want to force it down my throat, either. "Well, I think it'd be great if you could hear him speak a few times this week. His altar calls are definitely . . . unique. Vibrant. Different from the norm."

I shrugged, figuring it was a small price to pay for not getting in trouble for skipping. "Sure. I'll see what's going on, Dad. I'll think about it."

Dad nodded and smiled sadly, knowing through experience that was the best he'd get. He turned to go. Normally that'd be it, but for some odd reason I felt compelled to ask, "What is it, Dad? About this guy that's so special."

Dad gripped the doorknob tightly, giving me an odd look I couldn't quite decipher. "They say," he whispered in a hushed tone I'd never heard him use before, "that Reverend McIlvian's a healer."

With a brisk nod, Dad left my room, closing the door softly behind him.

SEVEN

I HAD MY first nightmare that night, of me kneeling at the feet of the good Reverend Alistair McIlvian in that clearing while he reached to the heavens and prayed in a booming voice . . . .

BOW DOWN BEFORE HIM, YE FALLEN ONES, SEEK SUPPLICATION AT THE DREAD FEET OF HE WHOSE CEASELESS ROARING ALWAYS AND FOREVER FILLS THE VOID BEYOND THE GATE, FILLS THE TIMELESS SKIES! HIS MIGHT TEARETH THE FOREST AND CRUSHETH THE CITIES, hear THEN HIS VOICE IN THE DARKNESS, ANSWER HIS CALL WITH THINE WHOLE HEART, OPEN YE HEARTS TO BE MADE OVER INTO HIS IMAGE, THE YELLOW KING OF YELLOW SKIES . . .

I thought afterward it was just because I was dreaming, but occasionally his words became garbled, voice grating with guttural consonants that didn't sound English . . . or even human, at all.

And the flies.

Buzzing and humming beneath McIlvian's chant, a droning undertone that seemed to rise and fall in cadence with his voice. The curious thing?

The flies were yellow.

THE MAN IN YELLOW

They weren't bees or hornets or yellow jackets. Their buzz was heavier, throatier sounding. No, this high-pitched buzzing could only come from flies. Bright yellow ones swarmed over the two dead skinned dogs, undulating in a pulsing yellow carpet.

And then, all at once . . . Reverend McIlvian fell silent. So did the flies. Everything in the woods behind the church fell silent. I looked up at McIlvian—the man in the bright yellow suit—with a curious mixture of dread and awe.

He loomed above me, towering, like he stood ten feet tall. His red hair blazed, as did his bright yellow suit. I couldn't see his face, though. Only a flesh-colored smear appeared where his eyes, nose and mouth should be.

"Are ye ready? To accept the offering of One Whose Name Is Not to be Spoken? Are ye willing? To be made over into His Unknowable Image?"

Despite the fear clenching my guts, I nodded. He reached down, his massive fingers spread. I could see that ring with the onyx stone set in it. Could also see the blazing yellow symbol on it writhing . . .

EIGHT

I WOKE, SWALLOWING a sharp cry, sweating. I reached out, flicked on the bedside lamp and sat up. Sickly yellow light spilled onto the floor, throwing the room into a dim glow.

Nothing.

Empty. No one except me, shivering and sweating in my rumpled bed, as it should be.

I blew out a noisy breath, covered my face with my hands, kneading my forehead with my fingertips. Already the nightmare had faded away, leaving me with nothing but a vague foreboding. I recalled scraps of images: those dead dogs in the woods, weird yellow flies buzzing all over them, and that strange altar in the middle of clearing. Something about Reverend McIlvian, also?

The nightmare's dread fingers finally faded. I turned off the lamp and settled back down to sleep. As I drifted off, however, two thoughts bubbled to the surface. One: I thought I'd finally identified the markings carved on the altar. They were, insanely enough, like the yellow sign on the onyx stone set in McIlvian's ring.

Two?

THE MAN IN YELLOW

Bobby Simmons had been in the nightmare.
Kneeling next to me.
Feasting on one of the dead skinned dogs, tearing at its rancid and bloating flesh like a wild animal . . .

NINE

I N THE MORNING I made sure to get up and out of the house early so I could avoid Dad. The eerie figments left over from the nightmare proved motivation enough to avoid any more talk about VBS and the good Reverend McIlvian.

Reverend McIlvian's a healer.

Luckily, I was successful. I'd dressed, eaten and hopped into Bobby's old 1975 AMC Matador before Dad had even finished showering.

It was a pleasant July morning, warm without much humidity. Bobby and I decided to hit one of the few sources of entertainment in Tahawus, our lame little mini-golf course. Done up in an Alice in Wonderland theme, it sported plaster statues of all the main characters: the Mad Hatter, Tweedle Dee and Dum, the Cheshire cat, the White Rabbit, the Queen, and Alice herself. Believe it or not, for such a dinky little golf course, the statues were actually decently done. They bore more than a passing resemblance to the characters from the Disney movie.

We were in the middle of our second half-assed game when Bobby changed the mood entirely. "Hey, Stu. You ever . . . you ever get tired of being . . . like you are?"

I frowned as I readied myself for a putt of epic proportions. "What do you mean?"

"Well . . . you ever wish you were just like everyone else? That you weren't . . . different?"

I snorted. "Yeah. Sure. All the time. If wishes were horses, I'd have a stable full of 'em. My very own herd of My Little Wish Ponies."

I expected Bobby to laugh nervously like he usually did when I got sarcastic about uncomfortable topics. He said nothing, however. Suddenly, the very air itself felt charged with a curious sort of weight. I looked up and, to my surprise, saw by the glimmer in his eyes that he was far from joking.

I straightened, thumping my club against the course's thin artificial turf. "God. You're serious, aren't you?"

Believe it or not, Bobby and I rarely talked about our disabilities. The subject just never came up. Or, I suppose it'd be fairer to say we avoided the subject as much as possible. Not by conscious decision, I don't think . . . we just subconsciously agreed not to talk about it.

Things were what they were.

And that was all.

I shrugged, struggling with my emotions, trying not to let them show. "I dunno, Bobby. Either God made me crippled and gave you crappy eyes and lungs or it was all a genetic hiccup and we got shafted. Either way it is what it is. There's nothing we can do about it, right?"

I looked back down to resume my turn, but before I could putt, Bobby whispered, "Yeah . . . but what if there was something we could do? Or something someone could do?"

Reverend McIlvian's a healer.

I stood up straight, dropped my club and waved for Bobby to stop, as if he were about to drive over a cliff. "Whoa, whoa, *whoa*. Hold it. You're not talking about Rev. McNuggett, are you? Tell me your parents didn't sell you that hokey 'he's a healer,' bit too."

Bobby looked away, ashamed, as if he'd been caught cheating on an exam. He dug his inhaler out of his pocket, stuck it into his mouth, triggered off a blast and wheezed, "N-no. Not really, not to my face, anyway. They . . . they were talkin' in the den and I . . . didn' mean to eavesdrop, but they said my name and I was comin down the hall and they started talking about Reverend McIlvian, what people say he can do and that maybe I should . . . "

A hot angry flash pulsed through me. Parents. Fucking parents. They were all the same. Bobby's parents were having clandestine meetings about how their near-sighted, asthmatic son should go see the "healer" in town. Just like Dad had subtly inferred to me last night with his little "he's a healer" remark.

I pointed at Bobby. "Come on. Tell me you're not thinking that . . . "

Bobby looked at me and shrugged. A sliver of surprise shot through my anger, dousing it as I thought, *Holy shit. He believes it. At least, he's thinking he might.*

"No way, Bobby," I breathed. "No way. C'mon. It's just another load of bullshit. This guy's just another fire'n brimstone 'Praise the Lord; HALLELUJAH!' preacher, just like we get every summer. He's no different than the rest. Just got a flashy suit and an accent, which makes all the old ladies go weak in the knees and impresses the hell out of the local yokels."

Amazingly enough, Bobby merely shrugged again and looked away. "Maybe. But wouldn't you . . . I mean, d-don't you . . . "

He coughed.

Stuck his inhaler into his mouth.

Triggered off another blast, breathed in shakily and continued, pretending to examine the golf course's statues. "Don't you sometimes wish you . . . we . . . didn't have to be like this?"

He looked at me. It was hard—very hard—to maintain my annoyance in the face of such pleading eyes. "Don't you wish we didn't have to be different? That we could do things like everyone else?"

I scowled and folded my arms. We weren't supposed to be having this conversation. This wasn't what we were supposed to talk about, ever. "Shit, man. I don't know. Yeah. I guess so. I mean, I sure don't . . . "

I gestured vaguely at my crooked feet and twisted, thin legs. "Hell, I don't *like* this. I don't like not being able to play sports like Dad did. I don't like not being able to run and jump like everyone else. I sure as hell don't like how my knees and ankles hurt all the time. But . . . "

I slapped my right thigh, grabbed what little meat was there, shook it, and met Bobby's gaze. "This is what it is. I sure as hell don't like it, but there's not a damn thing I can do about it."

Bobby stepped forward, running a nervous hand through his hair. I saw it then, glowing in his eyes . . .

The light of a zealot.

Of someone with *faith*.

"I heard Mom and Dad saying . . . all you need is faith. Faith, and if you come to his altar, you'll be healed."

Man.

That word.

Faith. Fucking useless, my whole life . . . but something everyone in Tahawus seemed to live and breathe, like it was air.

Faith.

Ironically, Dad had always blamed my lack of faith on himself. Mom had died when I was nine. Because the church consumed so much of his time after her death, we had drifted and become distant through my early teenage years. He insisted I attend church every Sunday morning and evening, but that was it. Either because he was afraid of pushing me away, he was too busy or he simply couldn't verbalize his thoughts, we rarely spoke about my faith. Nor did he *require* my attendance at VBS every summer, though always he lamely suggested it.

Honestly, after Mom's death we went our separate ways spiritually. I think he always blamed himself for my lack of faith because of that.

He was partly right.

He was to blame for my lack of faith, but not for the reasons he thought. It was the way he *looked* at me. The way he looked at my crooked feet and twisted legs. And the way he always quickly looked away, as if feeling guilty that he'd just been caught peeping in gross fascination at a circus freak show.

In a sense, he'd always treated my cerebral palsy just like Bobby and I treated each other's handicaps. He'd rarely spoken about it over the years, never once coddling me or treating me different. I'd always had to pull my weight around the house, even mowing the lawn, though he let me use the riding lawn mower. When we occasionally went haying with the Dents, it was always assumed I'd work the wagons like everyone else.

To his credit, Dad understood of my physical limitations without pitying me. Every now and then, however, I saw it, flickering in his eyes.

Shame.

Regret. That a former All-Star quarterback, point guard and pitcher could father such a broken, bent and twisted son. Believe it or not, I think it was worse for him that only my legs were affected by my cerebral palsy. I was only *partially* broken. I'm only guessing, but I think he saw it as a cruel cosmic joke at his expense that from the waist up I'd filled out just like him with muscled arms, wide shoulders and a deep chest. But from the waist down?

I'd been twisted.

Warped out of shape. Broken.

Reverend McIlvian's a healer.

That's what really bothered me about the whole "Reverend McIlvian's a Healer" thing. I'd always suspected Dad's shame, half-seen in his eyes at times when he thought I wasn't looking, but his statement last night? It played false with everything he'd ever said or taught me. It contradicted his claims that he "loved me just the way I was, just like God loved me just the way I was." It undermined all the times he'd tried to encourage me to take heart and accept my disability. His stories that I'd someday leap with joy in God's grace on two strong, heavenly-crafted legs in Paradise?

Bullshit.

It was all bullshit, because after all that he'd tried to tell and teach me over the years . . . .

Reverend McIlvian's a healer.

. . . deep down, Dad preferred a "new" me over . . . ME—

Bullshit.

"Faith?" I sneered at Bobby. "Faith in what? That God made me crippled like this only to send some half-wit bullshit artist to 'heal me' for His greater glory? Just like that Bastard hit Mom with a fucking drunk driver so He could show us His 'greater glory' and 'grace?' It's bullshit, Bobby. Either it's all lies, God doesn't exist and we ended up like this by accident and Mom got killed because life just sucks, or God made us like this and killed Mom just so He could prove how fucking awesome He is. Fuck that, Bobby. If that's His deal, if that's the 'faith' I gotta have to get 'healed' . . . no thanks."

Bobby stared at me, eyes wide and mouth hanging open. I didn't blame him, really. Even I shuddered a little at how cynical and hopeless my own words sounded. "Fuck it," I muttered, half-heartedly kicking my golf club. "I'm done with this shit. I'll be in the car."

Without waiting for his reply, I turned and shuffle-walked through the mini golf course and back to the car.

Bullshit.

It was just so much bullshit. And the worst part? What if . . . what if this guy COULD heal me?

How badly did I want that, too, deep down inside?

TEN

MY LITTLE RANT ruined the mood for a good thirty minutes or so. We wandered silently up and down Main Street, looking for somewhere to blow an hour or two. Nothing really caught our interest until we hit The General Store.

Yep. It really was named that. It pretty much had everything you needed for just about any occasion: hardware, housewares, linen, toys and books. After wandering our way through the store, using our mutual silence to heal the sores my little outburst had opened, we eventually made our way to its bookstore out back.

See, I may love rock'n roll and heavy metal, but I'm not stupid. I love to read, even now. It's one of the few pleasures I have left. Anyway, I was making straight for the non-fiction section, searching for a Paul McCartney biography I'd wanted, when we came across them: loud and proud, in a screaming yellow cardboard display at the end of the Philosophy/Religion rack.

They were hardcover and blazing yellow. The faced-out copies displayed Reverend Alistair McIlvian on the cover, replete in his loud yellow suit, leaning against a yellow wall in a yellow room. The title—in yellow, outlined in white—was the most ludicrous thing I'd ever heard: *The King Wears Yellow*. The subtitle added: *And You Can Too*.

I wasn't that surprised. Whenever we'd hosted speakers for our VBS who had written books or devotionals, The General Store had always stocked their wares. In a smallish town of a strongly religious mindset, it made good business sense. If this guy was as famous as Dad claimed he was, of course The General Store would stock anything he'd written. By the looks of the almost empty display, it'd turned out to be a good gamble.

Anyway, a sarcastic remark was brewing but before I could speak, I heard the click-*hiss* of Bobby's inhaler and saw him snag a copy. He stuck his inhaler into his front jeans pocket, opened the hideously yellow book and began flipping through it. I stood there, working my jaw, as if chewing a particularly troublesome piece of cud. Bobby eagerly flipped through the book's pages, which I noticed were gilt a glittering golden-yellow along the edges.

Finally I swallowed and managed, "Are you kidding me, Bobby? You're not actually gonna . . . "

Bobby shrugged as he continued to flip through the book. "I dunno. Looks . . . well, looks kinda interesting. Dad said this Reverend McIlvian was something else last night at church. Sorta makes me wish we'd stayed to check him out."

Astonished betrayal pierced me, but I covered it with my usual sarcasm. "C'mon, Bobby. Told you. Guy's not any different than any other pastor or missionary or speaker that's come through in the past ten years. It's all the same bullshit we've heard before. This guy's just flashier. It's an act, Bobby. An act."

Bobby flipped the hardcover over to inspect its back. As if I'd never ranted about it at the mini-golf course thirty minutes ago, he said, "I dunno. All my Dad kept saying was how *different* this guy was, that he wasn't like anyone they'd ever heard. Dad's not easy to fool."

I groaned. Bobby's Dad was about as easy to fool as a lemming. "C'mon, Bobby. Parents always say that. It's just them trying to con us into wasting a whole week listening to some windbag blow a lot of hot air."

But maddeningly enough Bobby wasn't even paying attention anymore, so intent was he on reading the book's description. "Hmm. Listen to this. 'We've all been mistaken about His true nature. He Who Has No Name truly wants to heal our broke bodies, wants to heal us inside and out, wants to make us over into His True and Unknowable Image. All it requires is letting go of who we are and the pain our infirmities cause us, the pain we so desperately seek to define ourselves by, and allowing Him the province to do His Unknowable Work in us, for his Greater Glory and our ultimate fulfillment.'"

I opened my mouth to offer another sarcastic remark when a fragment from my nightmare surfaced . . .

Are you ready?

To accept the offering

Of Him Whose Name is Not to be Spoken?

I pushed the thought away, however, and managed to dreg up vestiges of my customary skepticism. "Bobby. It's just the same shit as always. Same story; same shtick."

But Billy wasn't looking at me anymore. He'd turned and wandered toward the cashier, still reading the back of that book. He whispered as he walked away, "No. No shtick. This is . . . different."

An unfamiliar loathing for my friend curdled in my guts, along with another emotion I didn't want to name but couldn't deny.

Fear.

I eventually did find that Paul McCartney biography, even flipped through it for several minutes. But the words meant nothing to me, all blurring together into a meaningless jumble. I finally swore under my breath, tossed the book back onto the shelf and wandered around the small little bookstore some more, not really thinking anything in particular, letting my mind drift . . .

Until I came to my senses at the ringing of the cash register, and found myself holding my newly purchased copy of *The King Wears Yellow: And You Can Too.*

ELEVEN

I DON'T REMEMBER much about the ride home. Bobby and I barely spoke as he drove wordlessly, staring down the road, one hand on the wheel, the other resting on his copy of *The King Wears Yellow*.

And me?

To be honest, I can't exactly remember, to this day. I think . . . I believe . . . I must've spent the ride flipping through my copy of the book. Even that is still a mystery to me. How I could've been walking aimlessly through the bookstore one moment, scorning Reverend McIlvian and his healing powers, and the next unconsciously buying his book, of all things.

In a way, I suppose it makes some sort of sense. All my life I'd gone to great lengths to convince myself that I was "okay" with my handicap. Turns out I was a pretty decent liar. However, even though it pissed me off that folks—Dad included—had fallen for this shyster's shit, deep down inside? I suppose a part of me wanted that healing, too. Or at least, a part of me was curious, wanted to see if there was anything to it, if it were possible for me to be . . .

Normal.

Like everyone else.

That's normal itself, I guess. We all want to fit in, don't we? Scary thing is, after all this time . . . I still don't remember what I read in that book, or know how much of it seeped into my brain and affected me without my knowing it.

In any case, I finally pulled myself away from that book, snapping it shut when Bobby pulled into the gas station on Wolton. Gripped by a sudden desire to be elsewhere, I said, "Feel like walking. Gonna take the shortcut through the woods home. See you later?"

Bobby shut the engine off and his eyes seemed to refocus, as if his attention was returning from somewhere far away. "Yeah. I'm gonna go home. Read some of this," he hefted his book, "but call me. We'll hang. Or something."

I nodded and popped out of the car, fully intending on leaving the book I'd bought in Bobby's car. He loved it so much; he could have mine, too.

I slammed his car door shut, mumbled "See ya" as I lurched away toward the woods behind the gas station. Of course, though I didn't realize it at the time, I clutched that book under my arm the entire way.

TWELVE

OF COURSE, THERE were decent—if not really convincing—reasons for me not noticing that I was still carrying that book. Not only was I confused, annoyed and maybe even a little hurt that Bobby was buying into that bullshit, but in all honesty I was worried about him, too. Bobby was a lot like me. His asthma wasn't just some lame wheezing now and then, he had it bad. He got the kind of attacks that closed his throat right up. They could land him in a hospital under an oxygen tent if he wasn't careful.

I'm not gonna lie. My cerebral palsy is no picnic. Everywhere I go, I shuffle-lurch-walk. Running is tragically comic. At the end of every single day my joints throb, feeling like they're filled with jagged bits of glass. But, I can breathe. I can do things without gasping for breath.

Like that walk in the woods. I went slow and picked my way carefully because, as I've mentioned, my crooked feet tend to trip more easily than others. However, at least I could walk that path alone. If my joints started hurting, I could park my ass on a rock or tree stump and rest. I wasn't in danger of falling into an asthma attack and not being able to breathe. I could do physical things on my own.

Bobby?

Not so much. Add in a quiet, withdrawn personality and Bobby was far more cut off from people than I was. So all this "he's a healer" shit worried me in regards to him, especially the way his parents had been whispering around the house about it, the way Bobby was so hypnotized by that guy's book . . .

The book I was holding under my arm, too.

Reverend McIlvian's a healer.

"Who fuckin cares?" I growled as I trudged on, probably going a lot faster than I should've been, given my feet and the uneven terrain. "I like myself just fine, fuck you very much."

The kicker?

I'm not sure, even now, if that was entirely true.

I mean, yeah, I liked being me. I liked my rock and roll and heavy metal, strumming on my fender and my dreams of stardom. I liked my fashion sense: Salvation Army chic before it got popular. I even liked being "that guy" who slacked off in school and earned mostly Cs but was one of the few folks in English who actually understood The Merchant of Venice and read Kurt Vonnegut "for fun."

I liked fishing, tossing the football around with guys after school (pretending I didn't know about their not-so-secret "no-tackling-Mike" rule). I liked the old black and white Universal Monster movies that played every Wednesday night in the summer on a big white screen in Raedeker Park over in Clifton Heights. Even though I hated church and Sunday School because they were boring and hypocritical, I liked a lot of the old hymns because they had a 'substance' you couldn't put your finger on. In a way, I liked school . . . well, parts of it, like hanging out in study hall, cutting class; girls, of course . . .

But I liked me.

Mostly, I didn't want to change a thing.

Not even my legs, really. I mostly liked them just fine, in spite of the aches, pains, and how people refused to look at them. In spite of all that, I didn't want anyone messing with my legs because they were part of me, and that was that.

But, as I shuffle-limp-stepped my way down that path, those very familiar slivers of pain throbbing in my joints, I wondered how true that really was. Did I need my individuality that badly? Would it be so awful to walk like everyone else? Would I hate *not* feeling like my joints were grinding crushed glass every time I shuffle-limp-stepped my way around? Would losing my handicap really take something away from who I was? Or would it just make me better at being who I really wanted to be, make me . . .

Over into His True and Unknowable Image.

. . . who I was meant to be?

"Horseshit," I mumbled, slowing as I rounded a bend that also started to decline, "it's all a bunch of . . . "

"Horseshit. Aye, me boyo. Know how ya feel, I do."

I stumbled to a halt. Almost went down face-first in my surprise, I'm ashamed to say. I looked in the direction of that oddly lilting voice, realizing that I'd come to the clearing where Bobby and I had found those two dead dogs and that weird altar the night before. I also realized that, deep inside, I'd meant to come here the whole time, wondering if those dead dogs and alter were still here.

They weren't. The dead dogs and altar were gone,

but that wasn't so shocking. Someone else had probably cut through here since us, called the Town Board, and someone had come and gotten rid of them.

More surprising—and, maybe alarming—was the man in yellow, perched on a stump in the clearing. There, sitting with one leg crossed over the other, smoking a cigarette, sat the much-celebrated Reverend Alistair McIlvian, smiling at me in almost gentle amusement.

THIRTEEN

THE MAN IN YELLOW—Reverend McIlvian—took a drag on his cigarette, snorted smoke out his nostrils and pointed at me, smiling kindly as he spoke. "I un'erstand yer skepticism. Me own dear mowther usta spin me countless yarns bout His healin majesty'n grace, an that's whot I always said meself. 'Horseshit, Ma. Plain ole horseshit.'"

He replaced the cigarette in his mouth, puffed a few times, then said, lips clenched around his cigarette, "Course, things changed a wee bit intha war. Found meself inna bad place, lookin for answers, most often'n not intha bottom of a pint glass of bitters, or intha busniess enda my service revolver. We all come to Him in different ways, lad . . . an a right pack of us need to come to th' end of ourselves afore we'll give Him the time'o day. I spect many a soldier's come to Him in much the same way overtha years."

I frowned, feeling confused and wary . . . and I'm not ashamed to admit, a little scared. And when I'm scared, I get snarky. "Yeah? What war? You don't look *that* old."

Reverend McIlvian took another drag and grinned.

His eyes twinkled . . . and it must've been a trick of light coming through the branches, because I swore his eyes glowed yellow.

"Ah, but that'd giveway me real age, wouldn't it? Man's got to keep somethin to hisself. Sides, I dinnae wanna talk bout ME, overmuch. T'would more like to talk bout you, lad."

He took another deep drag, flushed the smoke out his nostrils again and nodded at me. "Yer Pastor Evan's boy, aintcha? Stuart Michael?"

Several emotions clamored for space in my gut. He'd of course interacted with Dad. Dad was sure to have mentioned his only family, me, maybe even showing the man in yellow a picture or two . . .

Or saying, my son, he's crippled
Can you heal him?
No.

Despite how Dad had acted last night, no way he'd do that.

"An sure nuff you an yer pal Bobby were th' ones peekin in on the balcony las night, after yer fine little walk through these very woods, here."

My breath caught a little as I suddenly remembered his unexplainable presence in two places at once last night. I stammered, "H-how did you know where we went?"

The man in yellow smiled big and friendly, waving off the question. "T'waren't nothin magical, lad. In the balcony I could practically feel ya breathin down me neck. Still got eyes inna back of me head, leftover from me war days, I suppose. An I saw you'n your pal slippin into th' foyer durin the openin hymn. This nice little path here goes allaway to th'gas station, an that seems a likely destination for two bored young men onna Sunday evenin."

Conflict swirled in me. The sun filtered through the tree's leaves, trickling summer heat into the forest's cool shade. It all sounded reasonable and logical enough. Except . . . except . . .

"How . . . how were you in the balcony? My father said you ended the service standing next to him, on the stage, so how . . . "

"How'd I be in two places at once?" Reverend McIlvian sucked on his cigarette again, then blew smoke rings instead of inhaling it. "A fine question indeed, lad. He Whose Face Cannot Be Seen works in mysterious ways. When we give ourselves o'er to Him, we find ourselves capable of many things. Just like Jesus, walkin on water, or after the crucifixion, appearin to the disciples in the Upper Room *while* he was also talkin to them fellas on the road to Damascus, all at once."

A thought crept up my spine on chill fingers. "You're . . . you're not just *here*, are you? You're down at VBS right now, teaching too . . . aren't you?"

Reverend McIlvian—the man in yellow, whatever the hell he was—smiled in a much less friendly way. "I kin see Pastor Evans ain't raised himself no dummy. Yer startin to grapple wit the big picture, now. Indeed, I'm meetin wit some of yer adolescents right now, talkin bout servin Him in their everyday lives. An I'm sittin right here, havin meself a nice relaxin smoke an a fine talk with you."

Something hit me, just then—an idea or notion— but it slipped away before I could fully grasp it. "How? How can you be in two places at once?"

The man in yellow cocked his head, his odd, slightly unpleasant smile still in place. "Many things odd'n strange are possible when we walk in His Unknowable Glory'n Grace. Mayhap ye'll learn that, by'n by."

He took another drag, the cigarette's tip glowing a bright yellow. He sighed and let the smoke trickle from his nostrils. "But, as I said . . . let's talk bout you, lad. That's why'm here, after all. 'Suffer th' children to come unto me,' as they say." He pointed his cigarette at me. "Don' wanna be rude, but I cannea help but notice yer limp. It's CP, ain't it? Cerebral palsy?"

I clenched my jaw. He was deliberately distracting me by addressing my handicap instead of answering my questions. I knew this, and it annoyed me. However, I do have to admit, I felt intrigued, too. No one had ever mentioned my handicap in such an offhanded way before.

"Yeah," I muttered. "Born with it."

The man in yellow nodded slowly, expressive face displaying what looked like genuine concern, maybe even a touch of sadness. "Thought as much. Me poor cousin had the CP. Had an awful time of it. Couldn' hardly get round, much less enjoy life, she limped so bad. Sad little thing she was, growin up. Never could play anna games with her friends or kin. No runnin or jumpin or ridin bikes or ice skatin or swimmin, even. She spent her childhood sittin on the side, watchin, pretenden she waren't always near to tears."

Hot anger shifted inside, rising past my collar, flushing my face. I've always hated manipulation. Can smell it coming a mile away. Right then, a flicker of

152

insight allowed me to see the man in yellow's concern as the manipulation it was. Quite frankly?

It pissed me off. I latched onto that like a drowning man clutching a life preserver. "I manage just fine, thanks. Don't need your sympathy, or your pity."

The man in yellow nodded, seemingly in complete agreement, which only pissed me off even more. "An right I can see that. You've a strong heart'n character, Stuart Michael Evans. A spine o' steel. Me cousin was the same. Have to be that way, I figure, what with the heavy burden you've had to carry all these years."

He tipped his head, lips pursed. "But strong as yer heart is, them joints'n muscles must hurt like the devil when the sun falls. Was that way with me cousin. Got so her joints ached so bad she couldn' hardly sleep, always wakin inna middle of the night, her thin an withered muscles always crampin up. She managed jus fine herself, too. Until she couldn' take it no more an put herself to sleep for good with a bottle a pills when she waren't just twenty-two."

The man in yellow smiled at me, giving me a knowing look. "But you don' look the kind that'll be swallowin a bottle of sleepin pills anna time soon. Seems to me yer the type who'druther leave this here mortal coil inna more . . . explosive fashion."

Right that moment, the entire forest fell still. All sound died. It felt like the man in yellow had razor blades for eyes. They'd just laid me bare to my soul, seeing all the nights I'd woken up because of cramps, rubbing endless ointments into my joints that never really worked, wondering about Dad's .22 . . .

I squeezed my hands into fists, swallowed and rasped, "What do you want?"

The man in yellow stood and spread his arms, as if his aims were so very clear, if only I could just see. "Stuart, me boy . . . to help, of course! He Who Waits Beyond has entrusted me with the greatest mission of all: to end pain. To heal poor tired souls of their wounds, their infirmities, that which makes em lackin in His eyes!"

Reverend McIlvian's a healer.

The man in yellow took a step closer. "I wanna heal yer legs, Stu. Heal yer friend Bobby's lungs'n his eyes, heal *so* many people. I wanna help you'n others ta be everythin He wants you to be."

Suddenly it was like hearing all of Dad's sermons about how God heals the weak and infirm. Blessed is the meek, they shall inherit the Earth, and all that shit. I'd never heard a "healer" preach before but I'd certainly heard the line about how much God wanted to heal all of us, if only we had enough faith in Him. The same old anger surfaced. Years of bitterness and even rage bubbled to the surface, momentarily pushing away my unease. I stumble-shuffled forward and jabbed an angry finger at the man in yellow.

"Yeah? Really? Same song, same dance, heard it all before! Let me ask you something Mr. Healer, same question that's always stumped everyone before, the question no one can ever answer. If God really wants to heal me, wants to get rid of my pain so bad . . . why the hell did He make me like this in the first place?"

I slapped my right thigh and snarled, "Why the fuck would God twist up my legs and hips if He could heal me whenever He wants? Why put me through all that? Wait, wait!" I assumed an expression of mock-awe, holding up a hand as the man in yellow started to answer. "I know! That's always the same, too! He crippled me and gave me all this pain and made me different from everyone else and made me shameful in my father's eyes just so he could heal me! He fucked me up just so He could show everyone His goddamn glory!"

That last rang out in the woods, almost hysterically shrill. In that moment, all the fight left me. I felt emotionally drained, limp and dead, relieved yet somehow ashamed, also. I'd just confessed my deepest, darkest rage to not only a stranger but a stranger I didn't trust. I'd revealed hidden pain that I'd never showed to Dad or Bobby, even.

I shuffle-stepped back a step. My legs suddenly felt very weak. They trembled, every movement sending sharp slivers of pain into my ankles and knees. Before I quite knew what had happened, I found myself sitting on a stump next to another tree, right at the clearing's mouth.

I shook my head weakly and looked away from the man in yellow, out into the forest. "Whatever. Bottom line, if God had to fuck me up just to show everyone how awesome He is by healing me, then God's a bastard in my book. I don't want anything to do with the rotten sunnuvabitch."

With that, I shuddered with a soul-convulsing breath and felt very, very tired.

The man in yellow chuckled softly, smiling. He took one last drag on his cigarette, dropped it on a flat rock and smudged it out with his heel. Smoke drifted up and around his head, looking almost like a halo.

He stood and walked toward the clearing's exit, hands in his pockets, still smiling in a way that sent chills rippling along my spine. Forcing my voice to remain steady, I snarled, "What's so fucking funny?"

The man in yellow grinned, showing evenly spaced, bright white teeth. "Well, here's th' thing. Who said anythin about *God*, boyo?"

FOURTEEN

I BLINKED AND jerked awake, nearly falling off the stump I'd obviously sat on to rest. A sudden weariness washed over me. I blinked some more, feeling very much like I'd just woken up from a long sleep.

I looked around.

The clearing was empty. The man in yellow—Reverend Alistair McIlvian—had gone, leaving me alone. Or had he ever been there to begin with? I yawned, thinking how unlikely it was I could've nodded off and dreamed the whole encounter.

I looked up. The sun had moved on. Time had passed. How much? Enough for the sun to move. How long had I slept, if in fact that's what I'd done? Was it late afternoon, early evening . . .

Sounds.

Laughing. Clapping. Singing?

Hymns. People singing hymns somewhere past the end of the path, near the church . . .

"Brothers'n sisters of His mercy, 'ere in Tahawaus . . ."

I lurched off the stump (dimly realizing I still clutched that book under my arm) and shuffle-stepped my way out of the clearing and down the path. I rushed as fast as my crooked feet would carry me without throwing me headlong. As I hobbled toward the path's end, my knees and ankles and hips throbbing, that booming voice seemed to grow louder with each step I took.

" . . . we should be honored to've been called to witness this glorious communion with Him, as one of your very own—a young'un—has chosen to . . . "

As the end of the path loomed, the voice seemed to rise and fall in pitch and tone, slowing down, speeding up, wavering between crystal-clarity and sluggish monotone. It sounded, at times, as if the speaker's mouth was filled with oil, the words gurgling and bubbling. Other times the voice echoed, as if coming from down a long tunnel.

I came to the path's end.

Slipped a little on a moss-covered rock and stumbled through the break in the undergrowth, falling to my hands and knees into the cemetery behind the church. My hands burned with scrapes and scratches.

" . . . an we are priv'ledged, dear brothers'n sisters, in Him . . . "

Him, who's Him?
Who said anything about God?

At the edge of the church cemetery I scrambled to my feet (unconsciously scooping up that book from where I'd dropped it) and stared, dumfounded. The sky had dimmed to early evening, five or six o'clock. More importantly, however, a crowd had gathered on the gravelly beach of Black Creek, which ran behind the church. They were holding hands, singing some sort of strange, ethereal tune I didn't know, one that rose and fell in a weird, rhythmic cadence that clashed against my ears yet tugged on my brain, all at once . . .

" . . . this most Divine Baptism, brothers'n sisters in the King, this baptism into faith and His Will . . . "

Who said anything about God?

And in the middle of Black Creek, clothed in brilliant yellow robes that blazed in the dim twilight, stood two figures. One had burning red hair and the booming, rising and falling voice, and his hand rested on the shoulder of a shorter, slighter, younger man. A teenager my age. The falling sunlight glinted off thick glasses . . .

Bobby.

Confusion throbbed in my brain. Couldn't be Bobby. I'd just left him at the gas station on the other side of the path, right? But if I had fallen asleep, that could've been . . . how long ago had it been?

Hours?

And during that time, he'd read the book. The book I now clutched against my side. Somehow, he'd read that book all in one sitting, being the prodigious reader he'd always been. Then he'd gone to today's closing services for VBS, answered the man in yellow's altar call . . .

Now here he was, about to baptized in the name of . . .

Him.

Who said anything about God?

I wanted to cry out. I truly did. I stepped forward, reached out, opened my mouth . . .

" . . . and I baptize thee, Robert W. Simmons, in His Holy an Unknown name!"

The man in yellow grabbed Bobby's shoulders and slammed him back into the creek. Growing up as a pastor's son, I've seen countless baptisms. They're usually gentle, smooth, over in an instant, but this . . .

The man in yellow *slammed* Bobby backwards into the creek and held him there. Bobby kicked and thrashed under the water as the man in yellow continued to hold him down. His hands flailed, fingers grasping at nothing.

The crowd waved their arms, chanting something that had no business coming from the mouth of man. I know that, now. This foreign and old-sounding language made me sick but also ebbed and flowed with a haunting, melancholy resonance . . .

The man in yellow looked up. Despite the distance between us, he stared at me, bright yellow eyes glowing under that thick shock of blazing red hair. He stared at me and held my best friend Bobby under the water . . .

The crowd chanted louder now. Arms waving and bodies swaying in frantic, almost . . . almost orgasmic release, chanting something I could just barely make out. One name, over and over, something that rhymed with pasture or faster or caster, something that sounded like . . .

Hastur?

The man in yellow looked at me, eyes blazing yellow. Even though he was two-hundred meters away I heard him whisper in my head: *amen*.

He released Bobby's shoulders.

Threw his arms into the air, looked away from me and screamed into the sky. There was no mistaking it, this time . . .

"Hastur! Ia, Hastur!"

Bobby's hands slowly sank out of sight into the waters of Black Creek.

THE MAN IN YELLOW

"Hastur!"

I cried out, fell against a headstone next to me, grasping it for support . . .

FIFTEEN

. . . AND JERKED UPRIGHT at the dining room
table at home.

My vision throbbed and blurred, making me dizzy.
Instantly overcome by a bone-deep fatigue, I yawned
and stretched. Rubbing my eyes, I looked around,
muddled, head fuzzy, trying to get my bearings.

I glanced at the sliding glass doors. Darkish
outside. Early evening. A look at the clock on the wall
in the kitchen confirmed it: seven o'clock.

I yawned again, ran a hand through my hair to the
back of my neck and rubbed it there, working out the
stiffness. Asleep. I'd fallen asleep at the dining room
table. I must've dozed for a few hours, judging by how
stiff and sore my neck felt . . . but what had I been
doing that put me asleep? Not school work, obviously.
It was summer. I did all my pleasure reading in my
bedroom . . .

I looked down. An icy chill rippled along my spine
at what lay open on the table before me.

A hardcover book with a yellow cover, its pages
gilded golden-yellow.

I bit my lip hard enough to taste a little blood. I
didn't look at the book's text. Something in my mind

shrank back from the notion. Inwardly I cringed at the idea that I might've read anything from that damn yellow book at all . . .

Maybe it's a different book; maybe it's a novel I checked out from the library, or . . .

I reached out, hand trembling, and with a finger—as if afraid of touching some deadly waste—flicked the book shut with a fingertip. The cover filled me with a creeping, ice-cold dread.

There he was, on the cover. Smiling and looking directly at me, it seemed.

The man in yellow.

Above that, the title burned itself into my brain: *The King Wears Yellow.*

"And so can you," I rasped.

I placed a weak hand on my forehead and held it there. Was I feverish? Sick, hallucinating? I hadn't bought that book . . . had I? I'd only glanced through it. Left it at The General Store, because it was just a crock of stupid shit. Hadn't I only flipped through Bobby's copy on the way home?

Until you got out at the gas station on Wolton Street and took the shortcut home.

Wait.

Got out?

Shortcut?

I did?

What had happened to my afternoon? Only fragments drifted around in my head. Miffed at Bobby for some reason . . .

No you were obsessed with reading the book and he was desperate to get home and read the book.

. . . I'd gotten out of the car at the gas station—

hadn't I?—and took the shortcut through the woods to think. I'd come to the clearing where Bobby and I had found those two dead dogs but they were gone and so was that weird altar, the one with the same markings on it as on the man in yellow's ring . . .

I closed my eyes.

Saw the man in yellow sitting on a rotted log in that clearing, smoking, smiling, talking but I couldn't make sense of the words. I saw myself hobbling down the path, slipping and falling, skinning my hands. I saw church members on the shore of Black Creek, the man in yellow baptizing Bobby in its waters, grabbing his shoulders and slamming him deep under water. I saw Bobby's weakening hands slipping beneath the surface . . .

I saw the man in yellow staring at me, whispering amen, and I heard that word . . . or that name . . .

Hastur.

The front door opened and closed. Numbly, as if in a dream, I looked up as Dad entered the den. He walked in a rolling, easy gait—as if everything was very fine in the world, indeed—in a way I hadn't seen since from before Mom died. He was whistling a bright tune. Sounded like some old time hymn from back in the day, and the look on his face . . .

Bliss.

Pure bliss.

Which scared the ever-living *shit* out of me.

At the table he noticed my presence, finally. He stopped whistling and smiled, his face turning slightly sad, like always, the bliss fading somewhat. He sighed. "Evening, Stuart. Didn't see you at the VBS closing services, tonight. Which I suppose is to be expected by now, huh?"

THE MAN IN YELLOW

Still dazed, confusion roiling in my head, I only stared blankly. He probably took it for my usual apathy, because he sighed again and shook his head. "Really wish you'd come before the end of the week, at least. Reverend McIlvian is something else. I don't think you'd hate it, honest. You might even . . . "

He trailed off, mid-sentence.

As his gaze fell on the closed copy of *The King Wears Yellow* sitting on the table before me. I glanced down at the book and then gaped up at him, meaning to shake my head, deny my reading it, even though I couldn't remember . . .

I didn't get the chance to speak, because Dad broke out into a grin the likes of which I'd not see in years. His eyes started shining. I swear to God he was on the fucking verge of crying.

"Stu. I'm so happy. You've obviously been asking yourself questions all this time, been searching for His Unknown Face in your heart. I can't tell you how proud I am that you're finally considering Him."

I couldn't say a word. I wanted to shake my head and deny it all, just like Peter did Christ, tell him he could take his fucking faith and religion and church and VBS and God . . .

Who said anything about God?

. . . and the good Reverend McIlvian, the man in yellow . . .

Hastur.

. . . and shove them all up his ass, but I couldn't muster up the words. I just swallowed and nodded weakly . . .

Then saw something under his arm. He followed my gaze, his smile growing even bigger, if that were possible. He pulled out his own yellow hardcover copy of *The King Wears Yellow*, which for some odd reason, finally moved me to speak. "Where . . . where's your Bible?"

Something flickered in his eyes.

His smile faltered. The corner of his right eye twitched. For a moment, his beatific expression slipped. A desperate, maddened face peeked out from behind those bright, shining eyes. Quick as could be, however, his mask slithered back into place. He grinned even wider, holding up that damn book.

"Reverend McIlvian's been having us read some passages from his book as supplemental study. Fascinating stuff. Very eye-opening." He nodded at me. "As I'm sure you're finding."

Again, I nodded slowly, my jaw working and my tongue twitching, wanting to say something, deny it all, mount some sort of protest . . .

But nothing came.

Because I had no idea whether I'd read any of it or not.

Dad's smile faded slightly. He became more solemn, looking more concerned, like he always had before the man in yellow came to town. "Y'know, tomorrow night Reverend McIlvian's planning a big altar call. He's been laying a lot of spiritual groundwork in all of his VBS classes . . . "

Who said anything about God?

" . . . and I think tomorrow night . . . well." He sighed yet again and gave me one of his usual humble, pleading looks . . .

But something hungry leered from his eyes. "It'll be a big night, Mike. A transformative one. Might not want to miss it. Also," he added, smiling, "Bobby Simmons'll be there."

My eyes widened, my breath catching.

The man in yellow grabbed Bobby's shoulders
slammed him under the water
held him there

"He will?" I managed, hoping I sounded surprised and not like I was choking on my tongue, which is what it felt like.

Dad nodded, grinning ear to ear, as if announcing the birth of his first-born SON, for shit's sake. "After you fellas came back from The General Store—where you both must've bought his book—Bobby spent the afternoon reading *The King Wears Yellow*. Then he came for the closing services at VBS, answered Reverend McIlvian's altar call, and made a profession of faith, pledging his life to Him."

Dad shook his head, still grinning like an idiot, face glowing again. "It was amazing. Energy filled the sanctuary. His spirit came over us, carrying us out of the church and down to the creek, where Reverend McIlvian baptized Bobby into Him, just like in the ancient times. You should've seen it, Stu. When Bobby came up from those waters, he wasn't sputtering or gasping at all. He was breathing strong and true. Threw his inhaler away, into the creek, because he didn't need it anymore. His glasses, too, because for the first time ever, he could see clearly without them."

I gazed at Dad stupidly, not understanding yet knowing what he meant, all too well. "What?"

"Don't you see? He was *healed*, Stuart!" Dad was getting excited now, gesturing with his hands in a way not unlike the congregation when I'd dreamed . . .

Saw
. . . the man in yellow baptizing . . .
Drowning
Bobby.

"Reverend McIlvian healed Bobby, son. *He* healed Bobby through Reverend McIlvian, through his Unknowable Grace and Mercy."

He looked at me, and just the way his eyes glowed . . .
yellow?

. . . I knew he was finally going to say it. Knew it even before the words came out of his mouth. "And he can heal you, too, Stu. If you'll let Him."

All the sarcastic, nasty, cynical things I wanted to say died on my tongue in the face of his near-weeping joy, his shining eyes. I couldn't do it. Not after the strange day I'd had, plagued by the things I'd apparently daydreamed . . .
Seen

. . . and with the way he was looking at me right now, brimming with such mournful hope and love. Believe it or not, I just didn't have it in me. Strangely enough, however, I was propelled by some unknown urge to ask: "He *who*, Dad? God?"

Again, that flicker in his eyes.

The joyful mask he wore slipped, revealing a desperate, mad look beneath. His right eye twitched as he licked his lips. Then he smiled and slipped his mask back into place. "Of course, Stu. Of course."
Who said anything about God?

Dad nodded upstairs. "I'm heading to bed. You should, too. Big day tomorrow. You'll need the rest."

He nodded once, turned and tramped upstairs, leaving me alone at the den table, staring at a closed yellow book, one I couldn't remember if I'd read or not.

A daydream.

Must've been. Or at least so I told myself. Bobby had stopped at that gas station. I'd left him, taken the shortcut through the woods home, got tired and stopped to rest in that clearing where we'd found the dead dogs that weren't there now. I'd dozed off on that stump, leaning against that tree . . .

But what about the book?

Did I have that book the whole time?

. . . and I must've dreamed the whole thing. Or maybe I'd woken half-way up, started down the path still sleepy and saw Bobby's baptism . . .

Are you kidding me?

Bobby, baptized?

. . . which Dad said HAD happened. Maybe I'd only thought I'd seen the man in yellow push Bobby under the water and hold him down.

But I didn't remember anything after that. Didn't remember coming home and reading the yellow book. What really happened? Why couldn't I remember . . . ?

Shaking my head, confused and tired and not just a little scared, I put my hands on the table and pushed off it. I stood on weak and tottering legs that ached, feeling like I'd run a marathon . . .

Or shambled down a shortcut through the woods.

. . . and winced, sucking in a hissing breath between my teeth. My knees and ankles throbbed with that old familiar pain, amplified a hundred fold. I had rushed down that path, hadn't I? I had walked home . . .

And my hands.

They stung, slightly. As if scratched from brush-burn. I turned them over, spread my palms and fingers wide, taking in the scrapes and cuts and small bruises on my hands, as well as faint streaks of dirt . . .

I fell.

I fell at the end of the path.

I closed my eyes and rubbed my face.

Somehow, I must've found my way upstairs to my bedroom, because before I knew it, I was in my bed, asleep and dreaming.

SIXTEEN

IN THE DREAM I was walking down the path again, this time at night. I shouldn't have been able to see much, but the moon above seemed strangely large and bright. It cast an odd luminescence that filtered through the trees, bathing everything in an eerie yellow glow. The path seemed different. Alien. As if I didn't belong there. It *looked* like the path running through the woods from the gas station to the church, but it also looked like it led elsewhere, somewhere different . . .

Somewhere beyond.

Up ahead on my left, I recognized the break in undergrowth leading to the clearing where Bobby and I discovered those two dead dogs and that weird altar. As I quickened my pace, compelled toward that clearing, I felt myself moving along the path smoothly, quickly, with purpose, strength and ease. I was walking with a rhythmic, even gait. I felt no pain in my extremities or my lower back at all.

I didn't look down at my legs, however, just marveled at how fluidly I was moving down that path. In fact, I quickened my pace, because as I neared the break in the undergrowth, I heard sounds that at once sent icy ripples down my spine and warmed my guts with the heat of . . . desire.

Low, jumbled sounds.

Mixing together. Chaotic, discordant . . . almost bestial.

Grunting. Snorting. An occasional whine or even a yelp or squeal, a snuffling . . .

They were *hungry* sounds. Growling, yipping and snapping. Even moans of animalistic pleasure spiced with panting huffs of breath . . .

The clearing was upon me. I stepped off the path, inside . . .

There he stood. The man in yellow. Smiling at me, holding his hands outstretched, as if he'd been waiting for me and only me. He stepped forward. When he spoke, thousands of clamoring voices hissed from his mouth at once, along with a low, droning hum . . . like flies.

Thousands upon thousands of fat, mutant, yellow flies.

"Join us," he buzzed with a chorus of voices, "accept His Blessing. Be remade in His Image. Join in Communion with us."

I stared at him, mouth hanging open. His eyes glowed a yellow twice as bright as his suit. His teeth glimmered a sickly, unnatural yellow. His face sagged, the flesh loose around the eyes and mouth, like an ill-fitting rubber mask that no longer held the shape of a human face. A nauseating thought bubbled up in my head: If I were to pull off the man in yellow's face . . . what would I see, underneath?

What did that loose-fitting mask hide?

I wanted to look away from that horrible, sagging

face and burning yellow eyes, but I couldn't. I saw, in fleeting glimpses that curdled my guts, *things* writhing around the edge of the clearing. Things neither human nor animal, neither one thing nor another. Things made of twisted, polluted flesh. *They* were making those horrible sounds as they twisted and snapped and mounted each other, all to the tune of their own squeals. Whatever they were or had been, they snapped and thrusted into each other in hysteric mania. All this I only glimpsed, because as horrible as it was to gaze upon the man in yellow, it was preferable to the abomination of flesh surrounding us.

The man in yellow smiled wider, revealing jagged, yellow teeth. He waved at the glistening, thronging mass of intertwined and clutching flesh. "Your brothers and sisters, Stuart. They have come to Him, received His benediction, and He has blessed them with His image. They are one in the flesh and one with Him—All in All and All in One. We are all in Him. He resides in us, making us perfect in His image, through His tender mercies."

He held out a hand sporting long, jagged yellow fingernails. "And now it is time to complete the offering. Join Bobby. Take your place next to him as an Invitation. Join him and us. Let go of your fear and isolation, come join us, become one with us and ascend . . . let go of your infirmity and accept His gift. Be healed of the flesh that traps and hinders ye."

Against my will, I scuttled forward . . .

And dread realization hit me, dawning into a numb, cold horror.

Scuttled.

Not shuffle-step-limp.

Scuttled.

Quickly, smoothly, like I was gliding along the ground rhythmically, my many feet and joints carrying me with strength and fluid purpose . . .

Many feet and joints.

Many.

A kind of sick revulsion . . . and yes, dark anticipation filled me as I looked down past my waist to see what had replaced my thin, twisted, handicapped legs . . .

I woke in my bed, screaming.

SEVENTEEN

AMAZINGLY, DAD DIDN'T wake when I screamed. In fact, I'm not sure whether or not I did scream aloud. All I really remember is jerking upright, heart banging, head pounding, sweating bullets and what sounded like a scream fading in my head.

After about fifteen minutes—during which my heart hammered like I'd just finished a marathon—no sounds came from Dad's room next door. No stirring of bedsprings, no creaking of floor boards, nothing.

Eventually, my heart slowed down and my hyperventilating faded. I managed a shaking breath and ran a hand through my sweat-damp hair. I tried to piece together my second nightmare that week. Like last time, only blurred fragments remained. I'd been on the path in the woods heading toward that clearing, from which had come a strange and unsettling but also arousing medley of growling moans, grunting, hissing and yowling . . .

The man in yellow.

He'd been there. His face had looked different, however. Like a loose-fitting rubber mask. I remembered wondering what he'd look like underneath if I were to pull it off . . .

My legs.

Something about . . . my legs.

My stomach cramped tight with an icy dread I didn't understand. I grabbed my blankets, but hesitated. Suddenly I felt very afraid of what I might find underneath. I dimly remembered my strange, gliding progress down that path . . .

"Fuck it."

I yanked the blanket back and saw my every day withered legs. A strange and unaccountable relief filled me at the sight of them. I glanced about the room, my gaze settling on the nightstand to my left . . .

. . . and onto *The King Wears Yellow,* open to the page I'd apparently left off on last night before falling asleep. Which, of course, I didn't remember doing at all.

I struggled out of bed, barely resisting the urge to smash the book across the room, because at that moment I feared even touching it, now.

EIGHTEEN

I T DIDN'T TAKE long to figure out why Dad hadn't heard me scream, if indeed I had. The house was empty. Six-thirty in the morning—way too early for VBS to start, but the house was empty. I had no idea where Dad was. I assumed the church. Where else would the pastor of the town's only church be during VBS? He'd left no note, however, and I had no idea when he'd left. For all I knew, he could've gone two hours ago, thirty minutes ago, or maybe he'd even snuck out last night after I'd fallen asleep. He always made his bed in the morning, so that didn't offer much in the way of evidence.

All these things tumbled through my head as I sat at the den table, staring into nothing. I didn't know what to think or feel. Three days ago, Bobby and I had skipped the opening Sunday night services of our annual VBS to get snacks from the gas station and to chill. On the way back to the church we stumbled across those two dead dogs and that weird alter with the symbol carved into it. Both of which vanished the very next day, no fuss no muss.

I had awful nightmares. Lost track of time. Maybe hallucinated things that may or may not have happened. Maybe read a book I didn't remember reading and barely remembered buying. Dad was all aglow because of some new preacher/healer guy that seemed more like a con man than anything else. My best friend Bobby got sucked up into all the nonsense like a fly in a Venus trap, getting himself baptized and apparently "healed," which didn't make a damn bit of sense at all.

My temples throbbed with a dull, pulsing ache. I closed my eyes and rubbed them, trying to push the pain and confusion away. "What the hell is going on here?"

My rasping voice only accentuated the strange, forlorn silence of my home. Nothing made any sense. Nothing seemed or felt real. Hadn't, really, since we'd discovered those two dead dogs and that altar in the clearing, and especially since yesterday morning . . .

When I'd seen that damned book at The General Store. The book I'd apparently bought in a fugue state and then read multiple times without remembering anything. The book that . . .

I opened my eyes, looked down and—feeling very little surprise—saw *The King Wears Yellow* sitting open before me on the den table.

I loosed a shuddering sigh. There it was. The book that, apparently, I couldn't get rid of. Something tore free inside. With amazingly little fanfare, I reached out and pulled the book toward me . . .

The phone in the kitchen rang.

Its shrill alarm jerked me upright. A shock ran through me. My earlier feelings of revulsion about that book returned, shaking off the blissful numbness I'd felt only minutes before. Like a recovered alcoholic who had nearly fallen off the wagon, I jerked my hands away from the book, pushed my chair back from the table and lurched upright. The phone was still ringing, and as I hobbled toward it, hanging up on the wall in the kitchen, the shrill sound seemed to take on an ominous undertone.

In the kitchen, my hand hovered over the ringing phone.

Stupid.

Pick it up.

I answered the phone. "Hello?"

Nothing.

A little static.

The crackling sound of the receiver being handled on the other end, so I thought someone was there, keeping quiet, for some reason. Also, water. Lapping against something. As if someone was holding the cordless phone while taking a bath.

A wheezing, watery rasp. Then: "*Stu.*"

I frowned. It was Bobby, but he certainly didn't sound healed at all. He didn't sound any better than the last time we'd talked. In fact, he sounded worse. His rasping gurgle and watery wheeze made him sound as if he had pneumonia or something.

"*Stu. Come over. Please. I . . . I need help.*"

Another phlegmy breath. "*Please.*"

It was a good two or three miles to Bobby's house. He lived on the other side of town. My ankles felt somewhat recovered from all my tramping around yesterday, but my knees still ached with faint echoes of that ground-glass pain in the joints. Based on past experience they'd hurt for several more days. Walking over there was out. "I dunno, Bobby. I don't know where Dad is, and . . . "

A thought occurred to me. *He's at the church. He has to be.* Which, of course, was just next-door. Looking around the kitchen, my gaze fell on the key rack hanging by the door, and, hanging on it, Dad's keys. Just like I'd figured, the car was still in the garage and available for use.

I hesitated. Even with his infusion of the man in yellow's brand of divine joy, Dad would still be pissed if he found out I'd taken the car. I had my license, of course. I'd planned on taking some courses at Webb Community College in the fall. Dad had been hoping to buy a used car so I could drive there and back on my own, but he hadn't found anything yet. With his car he acted pretty much like any other dad, I suppose. He always worried about the mileage, car accidents, insurance, something breaking, or me not refilling it with gas. He'd occasionally let me drive since I'd gotten my license, but only with his permission, and under strict guidelines.

"*Stu,*" Bobby wheezed on the other end, "*Please. Something's . . . happening.*"

He healed Bobby.

Fuck it.

"Hold on, Bobby. I'm coming."

I hung up and shuffle-stepped toward the key rack.

When I knocked on the Simmons' front door, it opened just a crack. They hadn't locked it, hadn't even closed or latched it. That bothered me, deep down.

The driveway was empty. They didn't have a garage. I didn't wonder where they were, though, because I'd seen how packed the church parking lots were when I'd crawled by in Dad's Buick. They—like Dad and maybe most everyone else in town—were with the man in yellow.

The house sounded weirdly quiet as I stepped into the foyer. Empty. Still. Abandoned, even. I'd just talked to Bobby a few minutes ago, however. He couldn't have gone far. Why would he want to? Why call me, then ditch? Besides, recalling his wheezing breath—which had sounded even worse than usual—he hadn't sounded like he could go very far.

"Bobby?"

Nothing.

I cupped my hands and called louder. "Hey . . . Bobby. It's Stuart. Where are you, man? What's going on? You all right?"

For several more minutes, silence. Not a creak or a step. Then, a sound came from down the hall leading to the bedrooms . . .

The bathroom.

A sound like water lapping against a hard surface.

The bathtub.

Looking down the hall, I saw the bathroom door ajar. No light coming from there, but . . .

The sound came again. Water lapping against the tub's sides, and another, louder sound. A BODY shifting in the tub.

Was Bobby . . . taking a bath? In the dark? What the hell?

I eased down the hall, for once grateful for my slower than usual gait. As I got closer, the shifting-in-water sound grew more frantic. A quiet, icy dread weighed down my feet. My heart felt heavy and a claustrophobic hand of fear closed around my throat.

A voice—more an impulse, really, than a coherent thought—clamored for me to leave, fast as I could, and not just leave Bobby's house. Get into Dad's car, point it out of town and drive until it ran out of gas.

But this was Bobby.

My best friend. He'd always been there for me. Had listened to all my bitching over the years about school, asshole jocks, preppies, stoners and slutty cheerleaders. Listened to all my complaints about Dad, his religion, the church and my legs and how much they always hurt . . .

As I neared the bathroom it struck me how much about Bobby I'd always taken for granted. He'd always been there, hadn't he? Had always hung out with me, offering to drive me wherever I'd wanted, do whatever I'd wanted, willing to skip church every Sunday night, always lending an ear . . .

How much had I ever thought about him? Considered his needs? Thought about his asthma, which banned him from sports as completely as my legs did? How often had I gotten annoyed at him for puffing on his inhaler all the time, never once thinking about how *he* felt about being chained to the damn thing? How often had I really thought about Bobby's problems?

Never.

Another unsavory thought (it seemed the moment for spontaneous, unpleasant self-reflection): how much of our friendship was founded on the comfort of knowing that someone else in the world was also fucked up, rather than actual affection? How much of my inclination toward Bobby was motivated by the relief in knowing there was at least one other weakling cripple in town to . . .

THE MAN IN YELLOW

I stopped in the hallway, resting a hand on the wall. One other. That's right. I'd never thought about it before. That's how small Tahawus was. That summer, anyway, there were only two kids who "struggled" with "difficulties" or "burdens" like a handicap or severe limitation. Bobby and me.

Only two.

Two of us.

And a thought from my nightmare surfaced. Something the man in yellow had said . . .

Take your place next to Bobby as the Invitation.

More splashing and shifting sounds pushed those thoughts away. I inched forward, grabbed the bathroom door's knob and eased it open.

Darkness spilled out into the hall. The curtains in the bathroom had been drawn, in addition to the lights being turned off. At first glance it didn't look as if anyone was inside. No one stood at the sink. No one sat on the toilet, and the bathroom was a narrow rectangle with nowhere to hide . . .

Except in the bathtub, behind the shower curtain.

As I turned my gaze to the bathtub, I saw on the floor clothes—Bobby's?—and in the middle of the jumbled piles, a cordless telephone. I took a step inside . . .

. . . and froze as a body shifted and rolled in the tub.

Behind that curtain, something wheezed. Water shifted again. The curtain trembled and shivered, its metal rings jingling against the shower curtain rod. Fish-belly white fingers curled around the curtain's edge and pulled it back, bit by shaking bit. Though every fiber of my being screamed GET OUT, I actually took another shuffling step farther into the bathroom.

"Bobby?"

No words. Just that bubbling rasp again. Those dead, wormlike fingers pulled the curtain back another fold, revealing . . .

God.

How to describe it?

I saw . . . something there. Submerged under a tub-full of water. Something that blinked wide, bulging, luminescent eyes filled with madness and a heart-wrenching despair . . .

I'm a little ashamed to admit I screamed. I lurched away from that thing rolling fitfully under the tub's water, stumbled out of the bathroom and back down the hallway toward the den.

The worst part?

While I fled the bathroom, the splashing in that tub rose to a fevered pitch, the thing thumping and slapping at the tub's sides, as if desperate for me not to go.

NINETEEN

OBBY'S FRONT DOOR slammed shut in the wake of my frenzied escape, a sharp crack disrupting that quiet July morning. Not caring if anyone saw me, I stumbled to a stop on the front walk, covered my face with my hands and breathed in deeply, trying to quiet the pounding in my head.

What the hell had I just seen?

In all respects, I'm thankful that to this day only distorted, fragmentary half-images remain of what I saw flopping in that water-filled bathtub. Those fingers, fish-belly white and slimy, had sprouted from a hand and arm of the same color. It had reached up from a body the same as it. Huge, bulging and reptilian-fish eyes had glared unblinkingly from beneath the water, and . . . and . . .

Gills.

Several rows of them, slits on either side of that . . . *thing*'s neck, from its ears to its collarbone. Gills, puckering in white skin, pink around the edges, fluttering open and shut in rhythmic pulses, bubbling . . . breathing underwater.

Thankfully I remembered no more past that. What I did remember was enough to grip my entire being in mind-shattering horror. Maybe even madness loomed in my mind.

However, the summer sun glowed warm and gentle on my skin. I stood there, my heart slowing. I rubbed my eyes with my palms, uncovered my face and looked around.

The streets and sidewalks were empty.

As were the surrounding driveways.

The houses sat quietly at this end of town, just as they had been nearer to home. Most everyone—as testified by the packed church parking lots—must already be at church, despite the fact that VBS wasn't supposed to start for another hour or so. Then, I remembered Dad's words from last night, from a time that seemed so long ago . . .

Tomorrow night will be special.

An altar call.

Lives will be changed forever

In His sight, in His Unknowable Graces.

A fragment from my nightmare floated to the surface . . .

You will be remade into His Unknowable image, as shall we all.

I remembered the strange way I'd glided down that path in my nightmare. Not shuffling or lurching on twisted legs, but gliding along at a strong, smooth, rhythmical pace. I remembered the faint rhythmical sounds I'd heard, in time with those steps . . .

on many feet

. . . the CLICKING sounds . . .

of many joints

. . . and how relieved I'd felt upon awakening to see my two withered, twisted and crippled legs instead of . . .

186

two
two crippled legs instead of
many?
Remade
in His Unknowable image
A brief vision shimmered before my eyes.
Bobby's been healed.
Of bulbous, reptilian eyes bulging underwater and puckering, white-pink gills. A wave of nausea rolled over me, clenching my stomach. My head spun. I licked my lips and tasted sour bile in the back of my throat.

Slowly, I shuffle-stepped toward Dad's car. When finally there, I opened the door and stumbled into the driver seat. I closed the door, leaned forward and pressed my forehead against the steering wheel.

in His Unknowable image
remade
in His Unknowable image
I thought of bulging eyes and puckering gills on a boy who'd been nearsighted and so asthma-stricken he could barely breathe without his inhaler . . .

Bobby's been healed.

. . . and a once crippled boy scuttling around smoothly like a crab on multi-jointed, chitinous and numerous legs.

Quite frankly, I almost passed out.

It was a near thing.

A thought—which had been festering in the back of my mind—helped me stave off impending oblivion. Bobby and me. The near-sighted asthmatic boy and the crippled boy. The two most handicapped kids in the whole town, basically. Two dead dogs in that clearing . . . a clearing we always used Sunday nights, and the man in yellow's words in my nightmare: *join Bobby in the sacrifice of Invitation . . .*

I sat up quickly, mind spinning. "Sunnuvabitch," I whispered, fitting together pieces of the puzzle, "Holy fucking shit."

Us.

Bobby and me.

The two most handicapped kids in town. Whatever the man in yellow wanted to do here . . . for some reason, it had to start with Bobby and me. We'd been targeted the whole time . . .

Set up.

By our own town. Hell, even worse . . . by our parents . . . by Dad.

"Son of a fucking whore," I whispered.

I reached for the keys, so intent on firing Dad's Buick up and peeling rubber out of town that I never noticed the hand reaching in through the driver-side window. By the time I did it was too late. The rag—soaked in something smelling medicinal—covered my nose and mouth. An instant later, everything went black.

TWENTY

WHEN I AWOKE I found myself lying face first on a thinly carpeted floor. My head pounded, feeling about twice its normal size, throbbing behind my eyes. I licked dry, cracked lips and felt my stomach heave.

I felt enormously tired. Fuck it all, right? I didn't understand any of this. Didn't understand why it was happening. How it could happen so fast. How apparently a quaint little Adirondack hamlet had turned into a compound full of crazed cult members in just several days . . .

Of course, you're assuming it didn't start quietly, long ago.

. . . I barely understood what was really going on beneath the surface of things . . .

We're going to be over into His Unknowable image.

. . . and I wasn't sure I cared much, anymore. My best friend or what remained of him was good as gone. My preacher Dad had not only gone full-on religious-nut-loony, he'd apparently set Bobby and me up as targets or even (fucking unbelievable) sacrifices to invite the man yellow into our town. If the packed church parking lots and the empty streets and houses meant anything, I was alone in resisting the man in yellow. How could I stop this? How could I do anything?

Fact was, I couldn't.

I was helpless. Whatever was about to happen—another Waco, Texas; another Ruby Ridge—I had no chance in hell of stopping it . . .

At least, no chance of stopping it and surviving at the same time. I figured the only way of stopping what was happening would be to go out with a bang and take them all with me.

The church.

Everyone was here (because that's where I was, in a store room behind the sanctuary). Everyone who apparently followed the man in yellow was here at the church, all in one place. The wheels started turning in my head.

Then the storeroom door opened. Someone entered and shut the door behind them.

"Well, now. Tis a sorry sight this is, to be sure. Seein ya laid low like this, all curled up inna ball like a baby. Hurts me somethin fierce, that ye've rejected Him to such lengths, boyo."

In some sense, the man in yellow's concern was absurd. I actually snorted. The entire town had gone bug-shit crazy in the space of two days because of this man. He'd haunted my dreams and nightmares. Had done something to my best friend Bobby, and was planning something for the rest of us . . .

Making us over into His Unknowable image.

. . . and here he was, still playing the amiable and gentle evangelical ambassador of Divine Good Will.

THE MAN IN YELLOW

A crock of shit, because I knew what he was, finally. I knew.

He wasn't a man at all.

I must've giggled a little at this (hysteria finally creeping around the edge of my thoughts) because he asked, "What'so funny, mi boyo?"

I sighed and realized that lying there and hiding behind my hands wasn't going to cut it. I rubbed my eyes one more time and then slowly pushed myself off the floor to lean back against the shelf of supplies at my back. "Nothing," I muttered, rubbing the back of my neck, looking around. "Everything. What the hell was that rag soaked in? Feel like I've been out for hours and got a hangover, too."

The man in yellow, sitting on the edge of an old metal desk, chuckled. His yellow eyes danced with mirth, which, oddly enough, made him look all the more human, even though I finally understood that his appearance was nothing but a lie. "Your apothecary. Well, your pharmacist, as ye call em these days. He had all the things we needed ta mix up a nice little dram of somethin to help ye cool down fer a bit. An sure nuff, you did. Been out for quite a few hours now, an it's almost time for the evenin service. I figured you needed the rest. Pharmacist says the nausea should wear off soon enough, which is good. Big things happenin tonight, mi boyo. Wouldn want ye to miss em."

Gritting my teeth, I forced myself to look at the man in yellow. "Big night, huh? Right. Tonight you're gonna do to everyone else what you did to Bobby. Aren't you?"

The man in yellow clucked his tongue and waved a

finger, looking regretful and reproving all at once. "Now that was a wee spot o'bad luck, that, you comin onta Bobby afore he was ready to see ya. When Bobby's done comin fully into His grace, ya won' be able to tell anna diff'rence tween him an the next man . . . neath the light o day, that is. Under the moonlight, however . . . that's when His Face shines through in *all* of us."

The man in yellow sat up straighter, suddenly looking firm and disappointed, but not necessarily with me. "No, that was unfortunate, you seein whatcha did. Your Da's fault, really. Left you alone when he shoulda broughtcha ta mornin meetin. He's always been a wee bit easy on ya, hasn't he? Ever since yer Ma died."

He shrugged. "Un'erstandable, really. An I'm sure yer Da has learned his lesson."

A dread chill rippled across my shoulders. Even knowing that Dad had a hand in all this; worry curdled my guts for his welfare. "What'd you do to him?"

The man in yellow waved my question away. "Nothin he wouldn't'ave asked us ta do of his own free will. Nuff to say he's seen the error of his ways, an is thankful for His Grace an Lovin Correction. Course . . . ya could make things far easier on yer Da, by acceptin Him an His Grace, too. Make things easier on alla them, really."

I swallowed, glaring at him, and muttered, "Bobby and me. We both gotta do it, don't we? Those two dead dogs were for both of us. I gotta join Bobby or . . . or you can't do to them what you did to Bobby. Right?"

The man in yellow smiled. It was an awful thing to see, because that wide grin hinted at more teeth than should be possible in a human's mouth. Also, the skin of his face seemed to be hanging looser, as if it *was* a mask hiding his true face. "Yer a marvel, boy. All piss'n vinegar. I like that, surely do. He likes that, too."

He pushed off the desk and sauntered toward me, holding up a finger, smile turning into a smug sneer. "Here's the thing, boyo. Yer right on *one* count. You'n a yer friend Bobby were offered as Offerins of Invitation, cause you were the two in town needin the most healin. But it don't matter if you deny His Gracen' Lovin Power. You'n yer pal were offered as payment. He Whose Name is Unknown accepted. What you do now is irrelevant."

He stopped, put his hands into his pockets, and damn him if he didn't instantly morph back into the role of compassionate holy man. "So b'lieve it er not, I'm truly concerned with yer well bein. It don' matter if you accept His Gift'r not. But I *want* you to accept his gift, Stu. Don' wantcha livin the rest of yer life as only half a man."

"Really," I sneered, my anger only partially fake bravado, "as opposed to what? A fucking crab monster?"

The man in yellow offered me an indulgent smile. "As I said, by the light o'day you'll no different'n any other man. You'll look just like everyone else, an feel stronger, better, whole."

I snorted. "Right, but by the light of the moon . . . "

The man in yellow nodded. "Yes. His Face will shine through all of ours, revealin His True Glory."

Despite my anger and disgust, I shivered. "Like in my nightmare."

"Yes. All in All, and All in One. What greater glory can there be than that?"

The man in yellow glanced at his wrist watch. "Well now. Tis bout time. Sure I can't persuade ye to . . . "

"Fuck off."

He tipped his head. "Verra well. Maybe not tonight; maybe not next week. But He's jealous, He is. He'll win yer heart, sure nuff."

As the man in yellow turned to leave, a curious impulse propelled me to ask, "Why us? Why come here, to our town, out in the middle of nowhere?"

The man in yellow stopped, hand on the doorknob. He turned and offered once again the most genial of smiles. "Why not? Why this town, why that town? Why this village, this hamlet, that colony? Why Carcosa, why Roanoke? Cause you was ready. You was ready an needed it, so I came. An that's all."

He paused, smiled fading. "We'll be invoking His presence shortly. Others will be joining Bobby in communion with Him. Ye're of course welcome to join us. An if ye're thinkin a leavin us this fine evenin, well . . . there's some strappin young men jus outside this door. I'm sure they can help ye with anythin ye need."

He nodded, opened the door, left the storeroom, and closed it behind him with an ominous and final-sounding click.

TWENTY-ONE

THROUGHOUT HIS ENTIRE talk with me, the muffled sound of hymns had drifted from the sanctuary through the storeroom door. When he left, the hymns rose into a crescendo, exploding into a chanting the likes of which I'd never heard before. His voice boomed in that strange language I remembered from my dreams. I imagined him striding up onto the stage, arms spread high into the air, yellow suit blazing with unnatural light, the flesh on his face hanging loose as the thing that hid behind it got closer to finally coming out.

I hauled myself to my feet, gasping at the pain exploding in my ankles and knees, gritting my teeth against a sudden surge of bile. Somehow I managed not to puke, leaning back against the shelf, gasping for air, trying to gather my resources for one last final . . .

What?

What could I possibly do? The man in yellow had covered all the angles. Had obviously planned this whole thing out long before he'd come here. Hell, he'd done it before, apparently, in plenty of other places . . .

Carcosa. Had no idea where that was, but Roanoke? *Roanoke*?

Really?

What could I possibly do?

I blinked and passed a hand over my forehead, which felt damp and clammy. Something occurred to me. A stray thought; a memory. Perhaps the man in yellow hadn't covered all the angles after all.

Several synapses clicked in my brain. Puzzle pieces suddenly spun and fit together. I stumbled away from the shelf I was leaning against, scanned its shelves for what I was looking for . . .

Yes.

I grabbed what I needed, shuffled over to the desk, and with my free hand started rummaging through its drawers. Part of me reveled in triumph (morbidly so, because this meant I was probably going down with the ship), but another, deeper part of me mourned. If Dad had forgotten about what I was looking for . . .

Then he was truly gone.

I searched through the first two drawers and finally, when I pulled out the third and final drawer, I found what I was looking for.

Seems to me yer the type who'druther leave this here mortal coil inna more . . . explosive fashion.

"Fuckin A."

I grabbed several of what I needed. Pushed off the desk and limped over the shelf against the storeroom's back wall, the ones storing old and heavy curtains that used to hang around the church's stained glass windows. I reveled in the pain wracking my ankles and knees, because I figured it would probably be the last thing I'd ever feel.

TWENTY-TWO

E VER SEE THE movie *Backdraft*, Father? By the summer of my senior year, everyone including me had. A good enough movie, it was mostly forgettable, except there's this scene in which one of the fireman characters mistakenly opens a door without checking the knob for heat first. When he opens the door, his ass gets fried by a huge gout of flame. A backdraft, caused by the sudden rush of oxygen.

Now, I'm not exactly sure if that's what I was trying to accomplish. Point in fact, I *didn't* end up causing a backdraft. For that you need a smoldering fire that's used up all the oxygen in a room. But hey—I wasn't a firefighter or arsonist. I was a scared and pissed off (but mostly scared) eighteen year old trapped in a room with no way out. The door was guarded and it didn't matter by whom, because I wasn't gonna be waltzing by them any time soon.

That chanting was getting louder. Weirder. The words all jumbled and mixed together, like from my nightmare of what I'd seen in that clearing under the light of a strange moon. Only it was happening out there in that sanctuary while I was trapped in the storeroom, waiting for whatever would come next.

So, I thought: *fuck it.*

I hauled those old draperies over to the door, piled them there and lit them fuckers on fire with an "aim and flame" lighter. Dad kept a bunch of them in that third desk drawer. He used them to light candles for special services, and to light the grills for our annual summer barbecue. I'd discovered them one summer when Bobby and I had gotten bored, looking for something to mess around with.

I'm not sure what I'd expected. That those draperies would flame up in a fiery whoosh, catching the door on fire, blowing it off the hinges? Something stupid and unrealistic like that, I suppose.

What DID happen was this: those draperies smoldered. The cloth was thick. Maybe damp from being stored in the storeroom for so long, and the fire didn't produce lots of flames at first. However, slowly and surely, musty smoke filled the room, making my eyes water and sting, making me cough.

It occurred to me belatedly that, judging on the strange voices chanting outside, folks in the sanctuary were pretty busy. It might take them a while to notice smoke trickling under the door. Maybe too long, and by the time they did notice I'd be long since incapacitated or maybe even dead from smoke inhalation.

However, I stood within throwing distance of the door, hacking into my elbow, eyes squinting against the acrid smoke, forcing my eyes open, trying desperately to be ready. I had one shot at doing some serious damage before I went down. I didn't want to blow it.

As fortune—or Fate or Destiny or Providence or whateverthefuck—would have it, cries of alarm shrieked to life out in the sanctuary just as I was about to toss my stomach's contents all over my shoes. I tensed all over, hands squeezing tight. I forced my eyes open, staring at that door.

The knob twisted.

Something on the other side snarled (yes, snarled, like an animal), obviously burned by the hot metal. A shoulder was laid against the door, crashing it open, smashing the smoldering draperies against the shelves and the drywall behind it. *Something* on two legs lurched through the door . . .

And I unleashed another discovery Bobby and I had made on a boring summer day.

A huge aerosol can of industrial strength cleaner I'd found on the shelf. I held the 'aim'n flame' lighter to its nozzle, triggered the flame, depressed the spray, and a fountain of beautiful orange-red flames engulfed the mass of deformed flesh lurching toward me, hitting it full in the face.

It stumbled back, flailing *something* that I wasn't sure were arms, shrieking and gurgling. It slammed into the things following it into the room. Engorged with a fierce sense of triumph, adrenaline flooding my veins, I limped after it, triggering off yet another fiery burst, filling the doorway with fire.

Of course this whole time those draperies had been smoldering against wooden shelves stocked with packages of paper plates, napkins, Styrofoam cups, construction paper and all sorts of other very flammable craft supplies. That alone probably sealed the church's fate. By the time I lurched into the sanctuary, that storeroom was engulfed in a fire that was quickly working its way into the church's structure.

I knew nothing of that as I lurched away, ersatz blowtorch in my hands, a completely different kind of fire blazing in my heart. To this day, I'm still not exactly sure what I saw. I'm glad for that. I have a hard time sleeping as it is. I imagine sleep would be impossible if I retained any clearer memories of that moment than I do. I can say this, however . . .

I saw . . . *things* thrashing in the church pews. Some still wore scraps of clothing. Some still stood upright while others lay or oozed on the pews. Though I refused to let my eyes rest on any one thing very long, I believe that whatever I'd seen in my nightmare had come to the fruition within in the burning halls of Tahawus Methodist Church.

I do remember the man in yellow, however.

He alone had retained a mortal shape. Standing on the stage, holding aloft in his hands what looked like an ancient book. He'd clearly been reading something from it. As I turned away from the things writhing and screaming in the church pews and stumbled toward the stage, he turned from the podium, holding out that old book . . .

. . . and merely looked at me. Face blank and expressionless, looking plastic, like the mask I'd come to believe it was. He stared at me and began to recite something I couldn't understand. As he did, the flesh of his face started to soften and run . . .

I flung up the aerosol can, clicked the lighter and sprayed him with fire. I held that nozzle down and kept the flame there and didn't stop until I'd coated him head to toe with flames that looked like the purest, cleanest things I'd ever seen.

The man in yellow, painted in vibrant shades of red

and orange, stood there and burned. No screams of rage or pain, no thrashing or wailing. He just stood there, on that stage, burning.

When the flames touched that book, it exploded. No shit. It leaped into flame and exploded. For a moment its flames looked bright green, as if something foul and poisonous was burning.

Horrible screeches rose from the pews when the book exploded, but I didn't look. I didn't dare, because I feared that if I saw what was thrashing and whipping in those pews I'd lay right down and let the flames take me so I wouldn't have to carry those images inside me for the rest of my life. In that moment, a stark clarity shot through me . . .

I wanted to live.

In my half-baked plans to set a fire in my prison I'd subconsciously expected to "go down with the ship." Even if I failed to get all of them, even if I died in the attempt, I'd figured that would be just fine with me.

Except it wasn't fine at all.

No way in hell.

I wanted to *live*, dammit.

In that moment, as hell burned around me, I realized that immolating myself just to escape the man in yellow was not an acceptable alternative at all. So I flung my improvised blowtorch and lighter away and shuffle-lurched as hard as I could around the front of the stage to the other side of the church. I gasped, crying out with almost every step, desperately ignoring the sharp blasts of glassy pain in my ankles and knees and hips, ignoring also the things shrieking in the pews.

I knew I'd never make it past the flames spreading

through the pews to the exit, but I also knew on the other side of the stage, steps led down to classrooms in the basement. A *concrete* basement, that wouldn't burn. If I could just get to them, maybe . . .

Somehow, I made it to the other side of the sanctuary. Just before I plunged down those steps, I risked a glance over my shoulder . . .

You know the story of Lot's wife, Father?

About how she made the mistake of looking back on Sodom and Gomorrah as she and her family fled, and was turned into a pillar of salt as punishment, because God had commanded them to flee without looking back?

Well, I didn't turn into a pillar of salt, obviously. But something else happened, Father. I shouldn't have looked back, because there, on the stage, walking toward me . . .

The man in yellow.

Encased in flames, but not burning. His arms outstretched, beckoning to me, his face a blurred patch of melted flesh that seemed ready to slide off and finally reveal what lay beneath . . .

For a moment, Father, just like with Lot's wife . . . I wanted to turn back. I wanted to forsake it all and go to him, the man in yellow. Somehow, however, I flung myself away, toward the basement stairs. Unfortunately, after performing so admirably under such trying conditions, my handicap finally reared its ugly head. My crooked feet caught on each other. I tripped, plunged downward and rolled down several steps before darkness claimed me.

NOW

TWENTY-THREE

FORTUNATELY NOT EVERYONE in town was at church that night. A scattered few— those devoted *non*-attendees our faithful little town tolerated—had of course been at home. Some of them were volunteer firemen. They were the ones who found me in the basement the next morning.

"Somehow I didn't break my neck falling down those stairs. The heat and the smoke of course rose and enough of the floor held and didn't collapse on me. I ended up spending only a week over at Clifton Heights General for mild injuries and smoke inhalation. I did, however, suffer ligament damage in my knees and ankles from the fall, exacerbated because of my CP. For several weeks I got around first in a wheel chair, then with a walker."

I sat back in the confessional booth, speechless, deeply concerned for the poor man's soul, wondering about his sanity . . .

Except.

I distinctly *remembered* the burning of Tahawus Methodist Church, the summer after my senior year in high school. My father had helped organize relief efforts through our church: donations, food baskets and supplies for the families affected by the fire. I remembered the story in the papers about how most of the small town's citizens had died and what a tragedy it was, because the fire had apparently been started by . . .

"Candles," I murmured, leaning closer to the confessional grate. "I remember reading about it in the paper. They said someone had lit candles for the Vacation Bible School services that night. Someone knocked them over by accident and didn't realize until too late . . . "

The poor man on the other side of the gate cackled, sounding moments away from full blown hysteria. "Oh, it was too late, all right. Too late. Too late for any of them. Too late even for . . . "

The man gasped. The shadowed profile in the other booth bent, as if he was doubled over with some great pain.

"Too late for what, my son?"

"Too late for *me*, Father," rasped the man, apparently Stuart Michael Evans. "Too late for me. You see, I thought I'd escaped. Thought I'd denied . . . It. Him. Whatever. Thought I'd been strong, that my cynicism had saved me. I eventually recovered. Couldn't stay in Tahawus anymore but that didn't matter because no one stayed there. Almost everyone was dead, the town finished. I bounced around for a few years, finally came here, got a job at The Can Man. I made a life of sorts. Wasn't much, but it was something, y'know?"

A mental image struck, just then. A memory of the last time I'd dropped off cans and bottles at The Can Man for one All Saints fundraiser or another, and the man who'd quietly taken my bag: a thin, blank-faced middle-aged man with a slightly cadaverous face and sunken eyes . . .

With a very pronounced limp, his knees and toes turned inward upon each other. The thought that I'd most likely seen this terribly troubled man at The Can Man countless times before, oblivious of his pain, grieved me deeply.

Such despair and pain throbbed in his voice that I asked, "What's happened, son? You say you had a life. What's changed that? What's happened?"

Silence.

So deep and absolute, for a moment I thought he'd somehow left without my hearing. But he shifted on his side of the confessional, and when he spoke next, it was in a voice so flat it could've been a lifeless recording over the telephone.

"I saw his face, Father. That's what happened. In that split second before I fell down those basement stairs, his mask slipped away and I saw his face. I thought it happened too quickly, that it wouldn't affect me, wouldn't change me . . . "

A deep, heart wrenching sob, as if from the very pit of his stomach. "But it did. Just took a while. It was lying there, waiting. The other day I was on the 'net in my crappy little apartment and someone shared a video-clip with me on Facebook from Youtube and it was him . . . it was *him* in that same yellow suit, looking the same as he did all those years ago, preaching out West somewhere. He was preaching and holding up that same book and I listened and couldn't stop and when I woke up the next day, I . . . I . . . m-my legs, they . . . they . . . "

He screamed.

High and shrill.

Though I've heard people cry and sob their hearts out, wailing in grief, I have never before heard anything like that scream. Stunned, I sat there, frozen for several minutes. I heard him struggling to his feet, heard the door of the confessional booth slam open. I stood, about to throw open my door, to call him back . . .

When I heard it, as he fled down the aisle.

A loud, rhythmic, insectile clicking.

The sound of something multi-limbed and multi-jointed scuttling away.

I collapsed back onto the bench, to my great shame, paralyzed by a cold terror I'd never known before. I sat there, half-cowering in silence for nearly twenty minutes until I worked up the courage to leave the confessional and return to the rectory. Later that night I passed into a troubled sleep full of men in yellow suits and things dancing under the light of the moon.

CODA

THE WELCOME SIGN for Tahawus is up ahead on the right. A glance at the dashboard clock on my JEEP shows that, indeed, it *is* only about forty minutes away from Clifton Heights. I find that hard to believe. It feels like we've been driving for hours. Of course, I've learned in my few years in the Adirondacks that the back roads feel endless, surrounded on both sides by thick, seemingly impenetrable stands of Adirondack pine. A thirty minute drive to Old Forge feels like an hour and half, most days.

As I slow for the turn-off, I glance at Father Ward in the passenger seat. He sits with Nate Slocum's journal in his lap, staring out the window. He's been quiet for most the trip. I don't blame him. His encounter with Stuart Michael Evans sounded harrowing. Of course, he's now telling himself that *clicking* sound from Stuart fleeing the confessional booth must've been his walker, and not . . . something else. That Stuart had suffered some sort of hysterical break instead of . . .

Changing.

Of course, a call to The Can Man revealed that

Stuart hasn't reported to work all week. A follow-up call to the landlord of his apartment over Chin's Pizza on Main Street told us he hasn't been seen there all week, either. Because he's a week late on rent—a rarity; he'd always paid on time—the landlord let us in. We found a small, cramped apartment reflective of a lonely, threadbare life. Nothing unusual, except that it looked like no one had lived there for a few days.

I flick on my right turn signal and turn off Route 30 North. The 'Welcome to Tahawus' sign looks like all the Adirondack signs, or at least it did at one time. Its maroon background has faded to a dull pink. Its gold lettering and edging is chipped and faded, also. It stands slightly crooked. Also unsurprising is the graffiti. 'Joy Rox My Sox.' 'CHHS, Class of 2000.' 'Live free, die hard!'

Given the circumstances, I fully expect to see 'CROATOAN' spray-painted across the sign in a shaky, eerie scrawl. Thankfully I don't, but that doesn't make me feel any better.

"You know what's odd?" Father Ward says quietly as we pull onto Main Street. "Fitzy and I have traveled Route 30 to Big Moose Lake to go fishing for the past six or seven years. I don't remember ever seeing the sign for Tahawus. Yet, there it is, plain as day . . . "

He gestures toward the back window. I nod but say nothing, because I know Father Ward isn't really looking for a comment. He's simply stating something we've come to know very intimately these past few years: sometimes we don't see things until they're ready to be found.

I drive slowly down Main Street, feeling strangely wary, even though I instinctively know that the boarded-up and abandoned stores and homes are empty. Something in the pit of my stomach tells me we're the only humans poking around Tahawus. However, as past experience has also taught us . . .

That doesn't mean we're *alone*.

I'm no stranger to this sensation. This isn't the first ghost town I've seen. Down in Central Pennsylvania there's an old mining town in Columbia County called Centralia. It's been deserted since their underground coal mines caught fire in 1962. Very quickly the town became abandoned. The fires are still burning today, so the town will never be rebuilt.

A native of Binghamton, I had a cousin who lived in Montrose, PA. He knew of Centralia, as most Pennsylvanians would. Growing up he'd heard his fair share of ghost stories about why Centralia had *really* been abandoned. The summer after our senior year (ironically, the same summer the man in yellow allegedly came to Tahawus), my cousin and some of his friends and I took an expedition through Centralia. Most of the buildings had been demolished by then, though some stores and a church and the elementary school still stood on Main Street.

We didn't find anything of worth (though it should be noted we explored Centralia at high noon). However, the whole time I felt the same thing I feel now, driving through the deserted, cracked and slightly heaved streets of Tahawus: the sensation of being *watched*. Measured. Judged by some elusive presence hiding just out of sight in the shadows behind me.

In Centralia, I told myself that sensation was an illusion born of the desolation and silence. Being a teen with an average imagination, I only half believed that. Now, as someone who's seen and experienced unexplainable things with no answers, I don't even try to rationalize the sensation. I just accept it, along with gravity and oxygen: we're being watched, and we're not alone.

A few turns past leaning, gray and crumbling homes and we're there.

What remains of Tahawus First Methodist Church.

I pull up to the curb and park, leaving the engine running. I don't plan on getting out. Based on how straight and rigid Father Ward is sitting, I don't figure he plans to, either.

Because say what you want, believe what you want . . .

The air feels heavier, here. *Denser.* The overwhelming sense of some presence watching us has thickened. Despite everything I've learned in the past few years about things that hide in dark corners just out of sight, I feel very certain that what lingers about the charred ruins of this building is pure, absolute—*alien*—evil.

In fact, I can barely look at the ruins, though there's not much to speak of. If it weren't for the empty sign out front, you wouldn't guess it was a church at one time. All that remains is waist high, charred foundation cinderblocks filled with likewise charred rubble.

The thing that bothers me the most?

The church's lawn.

Dead. Dry and dusty, showing no growth. Knee-high grass and weeds overrun the lawns of the abandoned homes. The foliage has begun reclaiming sidewalks and parking lots, even poking through the street's asphalt.

But not here.

Nothing grows here.

"I grew up reading a lot of classic horror, Stephen King, H. P. Lovecraft, especially," Father Ward says. "Dad did, too. He was a different sort of pastor. A little more relaxed. Anyway, there's a scrap of poetry by Lovecraft. Goes something like this . . . "

Father Ward closes his eyes and with a thoughtful expression recites:

The Thing, they whisper, wears a silken mask
Of yellow, whose queer folds appear to hide
A face not of this earth, though none dares ask
Just what those features are, which bulge inside.

Silence, for several minutes, until Father Ward opens his eyes and looks at me. "Chris?"

"Yeah?"

"Let's get the hell out of here."

I don't have to be told twice. I put the car into gear, execute a quick U-turn, and drive as quickly as possible—considering the uneven road—out of Tahawus.

About halfway back to Clifton Heights, Father Ward flicks on the radio and starts searching for stations, which is usually a lost cause this deep in the woods, especially with a factory-standard AM/FM radio. However, after our visit to Tahawus *sound* is needed to dispel the eerie quiet that's fallen over us. Even country music would suffice.

After a few seconds of Father Ward pressing *Scan*,

a station blasts in loud and clear. A vibrant, energetic voice booms . . .

" . . . *an that's why, me dear brothers'n sisters, we must lay down our infirmities at His Unknown Feet an accept all the wonders'n glories He has in store for us! He's ready an waitin to work His Grace and remake us inta His Unknown Image, that powerful'n great Father from Beyond Time'n Space . . . "*

Father Ward swears under his breath and hits scan again. The next song is a welcome relief, though also highly ironic, considering our return to Clifton Heights.

AC/DC's "Highway to Hell."

But I let it play on. Because honestly? Compared to what we're leaving behind in Tahawus, I'll take the hell I know any day of the week.

Because suddenly it doesn't seem so bad at all.

THE END

AUTHOR'S NOTE:

The real Tahawus—formerly a small Adirondack mining town founded in the late 1800's—is a ghost town. After its founding, it slowly dwindled over the years as its mines closed and reopened, and it was officially abandoned around 1996 when its last mine closed. I've played with its location to make it fit my story, and no church—filled with cosmic abominations and a man in yellow—ever burned to the ground in Tahawus.

Not that I know of, anyway . . . .

THE END?

Not at all

If you want to read more of Kevin Lucia's Clifton Heights, don't miss out on *Things Slip Through*—When a child mysteriously disappears from a small town and even his mother seems indifferent, it's time for the new sheriff to step in.

Or *Through a Mirror, Darkly*—Are there truths within the books we read? What if the book delves into the lives of the very town you live in? People you know? Or thought you knew. These are the questions a bookstore owner face when a mysterious book shows up.

If you enjoyed this book, I'm sure you'll also like the following titles:

Tales from The Lake Vol.1 anthology—Remember those dark and scary nights spent telling ghost stories and other campfire stories? With the *Tales from The Lake* horror anthologies, you can relive some of those memories by reading the best Dark Fiction stories around. Includes Dark Fiction stories and poems by horror greats such as Graham Masterton, Bev Vincent, Tim Curran, Tim Waggoner, Elizabeth Massie, and many more. Be sure to check out our website for future *Tales from The Lake* volumes.

Tales from The Lake Vol.2—Beneath this lake you'll find nothing but mystery and suspense, horror and dread. Not to mention death and misery—tales to share around the campfire or living room floor from the likes of Ramsey Campbell, Jack Ketchum, and Edward Lee.

Wind Chill by Patrick Rutigliano—What if you were held captive by your own family? Emma Rawlins has spent the last year a prisoner. The months following her mother's death dragged her father into a paranoid spiral of conspiracy theories and doomsday premonitions. But there is a force far colder than the freezing drifts. Ancient, ravenous, it knows no mercy. And it's already had a taste . . .

Eidolon Avenue: The First Feast by Jonathan Winn—where the secretly guilty go to die. All thrown into their own private hell as every cruel choice, every deadly mistake, every drop of spilled blood is remembered, resurrected and relived to feed the ancient evil that lives on Eidolon Avenue.

Flowers in a Dumpster by Mark Allan Gunnells—The world is full of beauty and mystery. In these 17 tales, Gunnells will take you on a journey through landscapes of light and darkness, rapture and agony, hope and fear. Let Gunnells guide you through these landscapes where magnificence and decay co-exist side by side. Come pick a bouquet from these Flowers in a Dumpster.

Samurai and Other Stories by William Meikle—No one can handle Scottish folklore with elements of the darkest horror, science fiction and fantasy, suspense and adventure like William Meikle.

Stuck On You and Other Prime Cuts by Jasper Bark— A word of caution gentle reader, these tales will take you places you've never been before and may never dare revisit. They'll whisper truths so twisted you can only face them in the darkest hours of the night. They'll unlock desires so decadent you'll never wash their taint from your flesh.

The Dark at the End of the Tunnel by Taylor Grant— Offered for the first time in a collected format, this selection features ten gripping and darkly imaginative stories by Taylor Grant, a Bram Stoker Award® nominated author and rising star in the suspense and horror genres. Grant exposes the terrors that hide beneath the surface of our ordinary world, behind people's masks of normalcy, and lurking in the shadows at the farthest reaches of the universe.

Pretty Little Dead Girls: A Novel of Murder and Whimsy—Bryony Adams is destined to be murdered, but fortunately Fate has terrible marksmanship. In order to survive, she must run as far and as fast as she can. After arriving in Seattle, Bryony befriends a tortured musician, a market fish-thrower, and a starry-eyed hero who is secretly a serial killer bent on fulfilling Bryony's dark destiny.

If you ever thought of becoming an author, I'd also like to recommend these non-fiction titles:

Horror 101: The Way Forward—a comprehensive overview of the Horror fiction genre and career opportunities available to established and aspiring authors, including Jack Ketchum, Graham Masterton, Edward Lee, Lisa Morton, Ellen Datlow, Ramsey Campbell, and many more.

Horror 201: The Silver Scream Vol.1 and *Vol.2*—A must read for anyone interested in the horror film industry. Includes interviews and essays by Wes Craven, John Carpenter, George A. Romero, Mick Garris, and dozens more. Now available in paperback, as well.

Modern Mythmakers: 35 interviews with Horror and Science Fiction Writers and Filmmakers by Michael McCarty—Ever wanted to hang out with legends like Ray Bradbury, Richard Matheson, and Dean Koontz? *Modern Mythmakers* is your chance to hear fun anecdotes and career advice from authors and filmmakers like Forrest J. Ackerman, Ray Bradbury, Ramsey Campbell, John Carpenter, Dan Curtis, Elvira, Neil Gaiman, Mick Garris, Laurell K. Hamilton, Jack Ketchum, Dean Koontz, Graham Masterton, Richard Matheson, John Russo, William F. Nolan, John Saul, Peter Straub, and many more.

The *Writers On Writing: An Author's Guide* Series— Your favorite authors share their secrets in the ultimate guide to becoming and being and author. With your support, *Writers On Writing* will become an ongoing eBook series with original 'On Writing' essays by writing professionals. A new edition will be launched every few months, featuring four or five essays per edition, so be sure to check out the webpage regularly for updates.

Or check out other Crystal Lake Publishing books for your Dark Fiction, Horror, Suspense, and Thriller needs.

About the Author

Kevin Lucia is the Reviews Editor for *Cemetery Dance Magazine*. His short fiction has appeared in several anthologies, most recently with writers such as Bentley Little, Clive Barker and Neil Gaiman. He teaches high school English and lives in Castle Creek, New York with his wife and children.

He is the author of *Hiram Grange & The Chosen One*, Book Four of *The Hiram Grange Chronicles*. His first short story collection, *Things Slip Through* was published November 2013, followed by his novella quartet *Through A Mirror, Darkly* in June 2015. He's currently working on his first novel. Visit him at: www.kevinlucia.com or add him on Facebook at: www.facebook.com/kblucia.

Connect with the Author

Website:
www.kevinlucia.com

Facebook:
www.facebook.com/kblucia

Twitter:
https://twitter.com/kevinlucia

Connect with Crystal Lake Publishing

Website
(be sure to sign up for our newsletter and get a free ebook!):
www.crystallakepub.com

Facebook:
www.facebook.com/Crystallakepublishing

Twitter:
https://twitter.com/crystallakepub

With unmatched success since 2012, Crystal Lake Publishing has quickly become one of the world's leading indie publishers of Mystery, Thriller, and Suspense books with a Dark Fiction edge.

Crystal Lake Publishing puts integrity, honor, and respect at the forefront of our operations.

We strive for each book and outreach program that's launched to not only entertain and touch or comment on issues that affect our readers, but also to strengthen and support the Dark Fiction field and its authors.

Not only do we publish authors who are destined to be legends in the field (and as hardworking as us), but we also look for men and women who care about their readers and fellow human beings. We only publish the very best Dark Fiction and look forward to launching many new careers.

We strive to know each and every one of our readers, while building personal relationships with our authors, reviewers, bloggers, pod-casters, bookstores and libraries.

Crystal Lake Publishing is and will always be a beacon of what passion and dedication, combined with overwhelming teamwork and respect, can accomplish: unique fiction you can't find anywhere else.

We do not just publish books, we present you worlds within your world, doors within your mind, from talented authors who sacrifice so much for a moment of your time.

This is what we believe in. What we stand for. This will be our legacy.

Welcome to Crystal Lake Publishing.

We hope you enjoyed this title. If so, we'd be grateful if you could leave a review on your blog or any of the other websites and outlets open to book reviews. Reviews are like gold to writers and publishers, since word-of-mouth is and will always be the best way to market a great book. And remember to keep an eye out for more of our books.

THANK YOU FOR PURCHASING THIS BOOK

CPSIA information can be obtained at www.ICGtesting.com
Printed in the USA
BVOW06s0122160716

455774BV00004B/17/P